SPINDLEWOOD BOOKS

No Roof in Bosnia

Els de Groen lives in Bennekom, a Dutch town not far from Arnhem. In the troubled last decade of the twentieth century she travelled widely in the Balkans and that experience is central to her recent writing. *No Roof In Bosnia* was short-listed for the Marsh Award and was the UK IBBY Honours choice for a novel in translation in 1998.

# No Roof in Bosnia

*Els de Groen*

*Translated by Patricia Crampton*

Spindlewood

Published as a Spindlewood paperback in 2001
First published in Great Britain in 1997 by
Spindlewood, 70 Lynhurst Avenue,
Barnstaple Devon EX31 2HY

First published in the Netherlands by Elzenga
in 1996 under the title *Tuig*

The translation and publication of *No Roof In Bosnia* has been
made possible with financial support from The Foundation
for the Production and Translation of Dutch Literature and
The Arts Council of England

Cover illustration by John Hurford

ISBN 0-907349-22-6

A catalogue record for this book is available from
the British Library.

Typeset by Chris Fayers, Woodford, Cornwall EX23 9JD
Printed and bound in Great Britain by
Short Run Press Ltd., Exeter

# Chapter 1

Aida was thirsty. Between the empty houses she could see an orchard on the slope above the village. Saliva gathered under her tongue. She had had nothing to drink for twenty-four hours. Painfully she swallowed down the saliva, already tasting the apple juice. Suddenly, throwing caution aside, she stood up from among the bushes and crossed the road to the first row of houses. She had no idea where she was. The village sign was riddled with bullet holes, like a flat colander. 'Bro..šte' she spelled out – one syllable was missing. She looked anxiously at the houses, and jumped as a curtain blew outwards, only to disappear again in the dark space of the window. The village was both eerie and familiar – she had seen several villages like this one, with black, scorched walls or ruined facades behind which tables and chairs still stood. The people had fled, but an orchard can manage without people. She could see huge numbers of apples, the boughs bending here and there under their weight.

Should she pick a few? She looked at the houses again. Farmers had warned her against entering 'dead villages'. They were smugglers' haunts and meeting-places for thieves. All the whispered warnings ran through Aida's head, but her thirst was stronger than her fear. She walked up into the village. At every step gravel and broken glass crunched beneath her feet, stones rolled away, twigs snapped, as if, instead of a path, she trod on a wounded man, who groaned at every step.

Suddenly a dog barked and she stiffened with terror. It was seconds before she could see the animal, seconds in which her right leg remained stuck in the air. Despite the coming dusk and all the chaos she could see the dog now: pot-bellied, bow-legged, like some ugly piece of furniture, standing on the front porch of a tumbledown house and barking, barking, barking. His loud bark hypnotized her, throwing an invisible net over her arms and legs. And when at last she freed herself and began to run away, it was too late.

'Napoleon! Quiet!' A woman's voice. 'Hallo! Who's there?'

The dog's name surprised Aida almost more than the woman who had appeared on the steps. Obviously no longer young, her round shoulders drooped, her grey hair was piled in a bun. She stroked and hushed the dog, looking round anxiously. Aida decided not to run. Exhausted as she was, she would see what happened and wait to be discovered.

There was no immediate reaction. The woman eyed her suspiciously and threw a swift glance behind her at the ruins. 'Are you alone?'

'Yes.' Aida's voice sounded very low and hoarse. She had to repeat the word, listening to the sound of her own voice. 'Yes, I am alone.' They were the first words she had spoken for three days.

'Come in,' said the woman, 'it's getting dark.'

As if the village were still intact, and the world normal, and Aida simply paying a courtesy visit to an aunt, she walked to the steps and from there to the house, one side of which at least was undamaged.

The dog lifted its upper lip and growled angrily.

'Basket, Napoleon, it's all right!' The woman turned back to Aida and pulled out a chair invitingly. 'Would you like milk? Or coffee?'

Aida's smile froze. She watched incredulously as the

8

woman began to grind coffee and then put biscuits, cheese, milk and apples on the table. Only the fruit belonged there – the rest was magic.

'Come on, drink,' said the woman, lowering her wide behind very, very carefully on to a kitchen chair, as if she were brooding eggs. She poured the sweet coffee into cups and said, 'To our acquaintance! My name's Antonia, what's yours?'

'Aida,' the girl whispered.

The two enjoyed the fresh coffee in silence, neither really knowing what else there was to say. The fat old dog scratched itself behind the ears with a rasping sound. In spite of the desolate surroundings, sitting peacefully together at the table had a refreshing effect on Aida. The tension receded from her body and under the table she pushed off her tight shoes, which pinched her feet. Then, hesitantly, she took biscuits, milk and a piece of cheese.

'I have enough.' Antonia had noticed her hesitation. 'I get this from the Blues, the men from UNPROFOR, and…' She leaned forward, chuckling, '…and I have a goat.'

'A goat?'

'Yes, can't you taste it? Goat's milk.'

After she had washed in a bowl of chalky water Aida went to bed. She had been lent a nightdress which was uncomfortably long and wide and smelled of the old dog. The bed was in a room in the damaged part of the house, where the walls bulged outwards, but Antonia said there was no fear of collapse. 'We have propped it up, you see.'

Who were 'we', Aida wondered. The Blue Helmets, the dog, the woman? Her thoughts rushed ahead, past this village, to the coast. Should she tell Antonia that she wanted to cross the border, or should she keep it to herself? She yawned and clutched one of the bed rails in order not to fall asleep, while she pursued her scurrying thoughts. Were the walls really propped up? How much further was it to the coast? Would she be able to cross the border? And should she talk about it or not? And were they firmly propped? There was a rumbling high in the mountains. Guns. Far away, this time.

When she woke up she was surprised to see the light coming in, not through a window but through a crack in the roof. The sun was already high, it was late. She pushed back the rough blanket and wriggled out of the nightdress. Her clothes were hanging on a rail by the wall. She took them down with a little shiver. There was a cross there too, which, like her stockings, her jacket and her pullover, hung at an angle away from the wall. How had she dared to sleep here? She dressed nervously, moved the partition from the door opening and rushed into the little hall, looking back like someone who has just escaped from a collapsing building. But nothing happened. Her nerves were shakier than the damaged house.

Aida sighed and wiped the sweat from her forehead, then went to the back of the house, where the woman had slept. There was no one there, even the dog had gone. She sat down, undecided. On the one hand this was a unique opportunity to get away unnoticed, on the other hand that would be cowardly. And besides, she was hungry – hungry and desperately thirsty! She looked at the kitchen cupboards. Where had Antonia's food come from? From the Blue Helmets, she said, but if they really did bring food, they wouldn't bring it here, where almost everything was smashed and no one could be living? And if the woman had lied, did not that give Aida the right to go through her cupboards? She had opened one door, then another, when outside a dog gave tongue. The dog! Aida sat down again: the door might open at any moment. But no one came, and finally she could stand it no longer. She got up to look for the woman.

It was a lovely day. In the sun-drenched yard stood a seat and a table, with wild flowers in a jam jar. Ants and beetles were scurrying around everywhere and a huge pair of trousers hung on a rusty wire. The ordinary objects and the sunshine softened the sight of the ruined houses, but the sun never shone here for long. Above the village rose a mountain which was already in the shadow of its own wooded crown and was imposing its green gloom below.

Aida began to realize that she was wasting her time. She had no obligation to the woman, still less to the dog. If they did not come, that was that. She would go to the orchard, pick as many apples as possible and keep going towards the south-west. Relieved to have made a decision, she knotted the jacket round her hips. Suddenly she was in a hurry, she must get away before Antonia came, otherwise it would be too late. This feeling of urgency gave her wings, but she had moved barely seven metres from the house when she heard voices. There were men in the village!

In panic she rushed back to the yard, through the kitchen into the hall. What mess had she got herself into now? What was going on here? What was Antonia up to? She was so tense that her ears hurt her. Two people were approaching the house. She heard light and heavy footsteps and recognized the dog's snuffling. 'In your basket!' Antonia ordered. Then came a strange voice, 'Is

11

that enough for two days?'

'Yes, of course,' said Antonia. 'But will you have enough for yourselves?'

'We could do with some matches, we're almost out of them.'

'Right, I'll find some.'

There was a sound of cupboards and drawers opening and shutting. Aida leaned against the wall in confusion, quite forgetting the treacherous slope. Once she stole a quick peep into the kitchen and saw a man, or rather a boy, with smooth blond hair, which he was just pushing back. She heard the two say goodbye, something metallic clattered, and the door closed. Then everything was quiet.

'Aida, what are you doing on the floor?'

Aida opened her eyes and saw the old woman bending over her.

'Who was that?'

'That was Josip, my nephew.'

'Does he live here?'

'He lived with me for a while, but now he's living somewhere else.'

'Where's that?'

'I shall only tell you if you tell me something, too. Get up and come and have something to eat. I have milked the goat and picked apples, plums and berries, and we have water again, too. Josip looks after that.'

Aida went into the kitchen and sat at the table. 'Can I help?' she asked, when Antonia set to work, but she did not listen to the answer. She was wondering feverishly whether it was worth saying more about herself to solve the 'riddle of Josip'.

## Chapter 2

Antonia could see that Aida was completely confused. She was as jumpy as an animal, ready to spring off at any moment. She was even bolting her food, and her reaction to Josip was strange.

When Antonia had recognized her nephew on the mountain path she had thought of telling him about her new house-guest, but she had kept quiet. To protect the girl, to keep him away, and the others too, of course. She had to be careful to keep her own life and theirs strictly apart, except for the days when Josip came to fetch food. For months, like a stout guardian angel, she had toiled and slaved to keep four other people alive besides herself. Not that she ever complained. She had in fact often thanked God for the weight on her shoulders, which had arrived at the very moment when she thought her life was pointless.

And now there was someone else stranded in Brodište, even younger than the others. Antonia kicked off her house-slippers and put on a comfortable pair of shoes.

'Shall we take a little walk?' she suggested innocently. 'I'll show you my goat.'

Aida glanced at her wrist-watch, which had stopped.

'Five o'clock,' said Antonia. 'My battery has run out too, but I know the position of the sun. Come on, or it will get dark. You've slept for such a long time.'

Aida stood up. It worried her that the old dog waddled out after them. She would have preferred him not to be there.

'Why is he called Napoleon?' she asked, to have something to say.

'A joke of my husband's. He gave all the animals names: the dog, the goat, our hens. But we ate them, they were not laying any more, and we were hungry. Did you know it was difficult to eat an animal with a name? Chicken and rice sounds different from Irina and rice, in my opinion.'

'Where is your husband?'

Antonia pointed with outstretched arm to an open space on the edge of the village. 'I buried his body, up there in the cemetery, and his soul – oh, I hope it's at peace. I hope it doesn't matter to God if someone was Catholic or Serbian Orthodox.' She glanced sidelong at the girl, with her aristocratic profile. The rising wind blew back her hair, showing her fine features to still greater advantage.

Uncomfortable under the woman's gaze, Aida scratched her forehead, hiding her face behind her hand.

'Who did this to the village?'

Antonia sighed. 'The Serbs came first,' she said. 'They searched Brodište for Muslims and set their houses on fire. They took on Croats as well. My husband shot into the house like a rocket, got rid of all traces of Catholicism and hung up an icon. That was how he cheated that trash. He was a Serb, you see. Was that right? Was it wrong?'

Aida shivered but did not speak.

'The neighbours, the few who were left, thought what my husband did was vile. The Croats called us arse-lickers, who only wanted to save our house, and the fourteen Serbs, the only ones living here, called us degenerates because we had a mixed marriage. There were three Muslims here as well, who were saved by a miracle, and they stopped talking to us.'

Aida's silence disturbed Antonia. Aida was a Muslim name. She did not want to hurt the child.

'My husband,' she went on quickly, 'took eggs, fruit and tobacco to the Muslims, but they simply turned their backs. "I'm a Bosnian," he said. "I've never done anything to you. I am a dentist, a doctor, it's my calling to help people!" But they never answered and that made the Croats laugh. In the end that was what broke him. He had a weak heart which could not stand up to his guilt feelings. I buried him up there, beside the church that lay in dust and ashes. And do you know the maddest thing? When I was burrowing a hole in the ground with my spade, the Muslims came and helped me. They bared their heads and said they were sorry. Jovo had always taken good care of their teeth. He had always been friendly, never superior or cold. They began to dig and asked if I would allow them to say their own prayers. They too were suffering from remorse. We covered up the grave together, and never have I been so happy and sad at the same time.'

'What became of the Muslims?' asked Aida. 'You're all alone here, aren't you?'

While they were talking Antonia had sat herself down on a low wall. She rubbed her thighs and stared into the distance. 'Soon after the Serbs, the Croat soldiers arrived, and this time the Serbian farms were set on fire – and two Muslim houses. The chaos was so great that the last people moved away. I stayed, but not because I'm brave: I simply had not the will to start again somewhere else. I thought, with the goat, the vegetable garden and the orchard, I'll get by.'

15

She stood up slowly, wondering as she walked on if it had been a good idea to talk about all those things. She looked searchingly at Aida, hesitated, and then said, 'It went well at first. I used to talk to Napoleon or Svetlana, the goat, but…gradually I began talking to anything that had paws or wings. I was well on the way to going completely mad. That was when Josip came. He had escaped from Sarajevo in order to hide here in Brodište with a friend. He had meant to ask for my help, but in reality he helped me.'

Embarrassed by what she had heard, Aida did not ask about Josip. Why had he gone away again? Just as she was nerving herself to ask, Antonia touched her arm and cried, 'Look, there's Svetlana!'

In a meadow beside the orchard stood a little white goat which suddenly stopped grazing and ran towards them until the cord that tethered her was taut. Antonia stroked the animal and playfully tugged her beard. 'Hallo, my girl. Got enough water?' She checked the water-trough, a bathtub hauled up from the village. 'I'll fill it up for you tonight, all right?'

She turned a laughing face to Aida. 'If anyone had prophesied when I was young that I would one day be milking a goat every day like a farmer, I would have laughed aloud. I went to university in Sarajevo. Do you know Sarajevo?'

'A bit.'

'A beautiful town,' said Antonia. 'I came from a village originally and I had nice parents, but they never agreed, and then they would quarrel. My student years were a release! In Sarajevo everyone has a mind of his own, too, but they don't fight about it. That would be pointless, with all those religions and nationalities.'

Aida looked across at the mountain behind which the sun had vanished. Only its reflection in the clouds above the peak sent a little light over the top, outlining the village before it melted into the background of the mountain. It was too late to go any further. She had slept the day away.

'Where are you heading?' asked Antonia.

'South-west, to the coast.'

'Over the frontier, you mean, and alone?'

Aida nodded.

'Dangerous,' said Antonia, catching her breath. 'The boys don't dare to do it, though there are two of them. There are smugglers, madmen and muggers everywhere. Wait until you get a lift.'

'But who from?'

Antonia waved towards the road. 'Sometimes UN convoys come along here with Blue Helmets. Brodište is on a back road which they take when the main road is too risky or not passable. They know me, they always stop. Next time I'll ask if they will take you along. All right?'

'How long would that be?'

'I'm expecting one any moment, but that one will be travelling north and you need one that will take you to the coast. You will have to wait for that.'

'How long?' Aida persisted.

'Ten days – a fortnight, at most.'

'Do I have to go back into that room?'

'Josip and one or two other boys propped it up.'

'Couldn't I just stay in the kitchen?'

Antonia bit her lip. She knew she would have to

17

answer. This was something she would not be able to keep from the girl even for three days. 'Listen,' she said, clearing her throat – she was a chain-smoker and her voice tended to crack, especially when she whispered. 'The quiet here is deceptive. There are militias fighting again to the north, Chetniks sometimes look in, sometimes Croats. Not ordinary soldiers, but guerrillas in camouflage gear. They call me the madwoman of Brodište and believe me, I do my best to seem as mad as possible. I've already had some experience. Only, they don't trust me. Sometimes I think they take me for a liaison officer.'

'But…'

'Yes, such rubbish, but from their angle not as foolish as it sounds. After all, what is an old woman like me doing here in these ruins? And where do I get food? Do I pay something in return and if so, to whom? That's why I put you in the damaged part of the house.'

'But do they come to your house, and who comes, exactly?'

'Their commanders, their leaders, mostly only one or two men. Sometimes Croats, another time Chetniks. It depends on the front line and that's always moving.'

'Do they come at night as well?'

'That has happened once or twice, but you don't need to worry. I give them something to drink and chatter away as only women can. And they never look round the back.'

Not yet, anyway, thought Aida.


They walked back to the house behind the panting dog. Antonia lit an oil lamp and gave Napoleon something to drink. From a plastic jerry can she poured crystal-clear water into a dented bowl. The dog pushed his muzzle in before she had filled it. 'Shame on you, Napoleon!' The dog looked up at her guiltily and shook the drops from his coat. Antonia laughed, but Aida did not. She sat grumpily at the table, jealous of a dog for the first time in her life.

'Drink up, there's plenty here,' said Antonia, setting a full jug on the table. 'The water comes from high up in the mountains. I get fresh water every other day, the boys take care of that.' She smiled when Aida filled her glass. The girl had calmed down, the walk had done her good, even if what she had heard was not easy to digest.

'You know...' Antonia paused, her face stiffening, tense with an emotion she had not shown up to now: fear. 'You know, I am sometimes so afraid that Napoleon will drink from the stream down here in the village. It's poisoned, there are a couple of containers rusting away in the mud, and a lot of animals have died already.'

Suddenly Aida knew how indispensible the dog was. She hid her flushed face in the glass, which she emptied in a single draught. Never again would she think badly of the poor creature.

The mountain water was cool and tasted of iron. Did Josip also come down from the mountain? She did not dare to ask that as well, at least until she had said something about herself. But where should she start? With the summons? With the bus ride? She needed something to start her off. She gazed silently at Antonia, who nodded, but asked no questions. She went off to take water to the goat.

# Chapter 3

Taking care not to spill a drop of the precious milk, Josip climbed back up the mountain path. He felt an irresistible desire to put the can to his mouth – just for a moment. He would count his swallows and subtract them from his share.

'Caught you!' someone shouted triumphantly.

Josip started and choked, coughing so violently that he had to sit down on the path. The milk slopped over the rim of the can, which nearly overturned, but two sunburned hands grabbed it in time. Haris had been waiting for Josip. 'Stupid, look what you've done! You almost did for our protein ration!'

'I was scared rotten.'

'Because you were drinking.'

'Because you shouted, idiot!'

'Because you were drinking,' said Haris.

The boys looked at each other and laughed. Haris was shorter and darker than Josip. He had an angular, rather surly face which could change with surprising speed from a childlike candour to adult seriousness.

'Well, how was it down there!'

'Oh, as usual. I've got matches and a piece of cheese – not a big one.'

'There was something down there. Out with it.'

'The milk will go off, man.'

'Not if you talk fast.'

Josip looked down at the village, which from here looked like a quarry or a rubbish tip. 'She was nervous, I saw that as soon as I arrived, and I asked if she had had any other visits, like last week. She said no, and went on about her onions. She has made a vegetable garden somewhere near the orchard. Then we went to Svetlana and I asked whether I should bring the jerry cans into the kitchen, but no, I was to stay with her, because she saw me so rarely. It was only when she had finished milking that we went to her house and then I realized what was wrong. She didn't want to let me in, but I had already seen the girl. Yes, it's true, a girl with long hair, about fifteen. She ran into the kitchen just before me. My aunt is hiding her.'

'Did you ask why?'

Josip stared in astonishment at his friend, who could reduce the most complicated matters to a question that he had forgotten to ask. 'Hey, listen,' he said, 'she must have some reason for hiding the girl.'

'Of course,' said Haris, 'but what was your reason for not letting her know that you know she is hiding her!'

Josip sighed. 'Come on, the milk will go sour.' They stood up and went on climbing in silence. The mountain on which they had their camp was called 'Gora', which meant simply 'mountain'. Huge, green and majestic, it rose towards the sky, so plainly nothing but a mountain that the people had not even thought of using names like 'Old 'un', 'Giant' or 'Baldy'. 'Mountain', they said respectfully.

The steep track widened out into a meadow on which they could walk side by side again.

'Hey!' Haris grasped Josip by the arm. 'You must ask your aunt. She's got enough on her plate. There's no room for another secret.'

'What if she doesn't want to talk about it!'

'Then she won't talk,' said Haris. 'We can't force her, after all. I'm curious to know who she's taken into her house now, but that's not the point. The point is that she knows you and I are on her side. She is in danger, and so is the girl.'

'You're not serious!' Josip teased him, and shook Haris's hand from his arm. They were out in the sun again, sticky with sweat, though it was not the heat that had made Josip irritable but the fact that Haris was right. He should have asked his aunt at once who the girl was.

Probably he had not done so because the girl's presence had taken him completely by surprise. He had seen her slip away like a shadow. Did she really exist? He had tried to look into the hall from the kitchen, but Antonia had pushed him with gentle strength towards the door. 'Here, cheese, milk, matches, and the rest on Thursday!' And before he knew it he was outside again. He had gone off, confused, although he could easily have thought of an excuse to return to the house. 'Oh, Antonia, we're out of candles, too! Hey…have you got a guest?'

He had not done so for a reason that Haris did not know. Josip was scared of his aunt. At home Antonia had always been spoken of with great respect: a woman with ambition, versatile, educated. Secretly he had revered his aunt, who resembled to a T his own mother, her younger sister. But Josip's mother was weak and uncertain, almost neurotic, whereas Antonia was strong. For years she had been headmistress of a girls' high school, when, aged about 40, she began a relationship with a man, resigned her position, married and moved to the country. The whole family had been surprised, but

23

not worried. Antonia knew what she wanted. With the same calm with which she had run her school, she embarked on her marriage to Jovo, a Serbian dentist, and then came the shock of this spring, shortly after Haris and Josip had fled to his aunt from the beleaguered capital.

They had found her sitting, inert and sick, on a chair in a ruined house, where a chained dog had almost throttled itself trying to attack them. Josip and Haris had been unable to speak, but she, the last inhabitant of Brodište, had smiled without recognising them. Josip would never forget that terrible and painful scene, and he still remembered what she had said, 'Are you coming to school here?' So there she sat, his brilliant, idolized aunt, just as sick as his own mother. With Haris he had fetched water from a mountain stream, not from the village stream which was no good. She had begun to scream hysterically, 'The stream in the village has been poisoned!' So they had washed the floor tiles, sink, dog, clothes, bedding, pots and all the windows that were still whole, with mountain water. They had worked like horses while the woman came to herself again.

Antonia had grown a little more normal every day, until in the summer she looked the same as ever, but Josip could not forget those images from the spring. However bravely Antonia behaved, and however well she looked after herself, he was always afraid that the sickness would return. So he chose his words carefully, always watching her face, especially when he was trying to persuade her to leave the village, which he did more and more often. That was why he had not had the courage to ask about the girl.

24

They were standing high up on the mountain now, a pleasant breeze blowing through their hair.

'Why so quiet?' said Haris.

Josip shrugged. His eyes moved thoughtfully across the southern slope of the mountain to the cave they lived in.

'We won't say anything to them,' said Haris. 'All right? First of all we must find out who your aunt is hiding.'

'How?' asked Josip.

'I'll go down with you the day after tomorrow, a bit earlier than usual, or later, perhaps – anyway, when we're not expected.'

'Sneaky,' said Josip, but he knew that was nonsense. In all the world there wasn't a boy more honest than Haris. Nor more eccentric, for that matter!

Svetlana was tethered by a very long rope so that she could move quite freely about the meadow, but sometimes Antonia shut her in. When there was a growling in the mountains and a storm or something worse was approaching, the goat was moved to a hut camouflaged with branches. Antonia missed nothing, she was on the alert night and day – until that spring, when the goat had almost died of thirst and Napoleon had to do battle alone with an army of fleas. She hated to remember that time and was ashamed when she thought of the boys, whom she was now trying to help as they had helped her.

After Haris and Josip, Mila and Ramiz had arrived. Aida was the fifth.

Once again Antonia had persuaded her to come for a

walk. She had noticed that the girl was calmer outside than indoors. They strolled together past the rectangular onion and potato patches, the parsley and delicate little tomato plants. 'If my harvest fails,' said Antonia, 'I shall have to get through the winter with stewed wild fruit, but for that I need sugar.'

'I don't know anything about that,' said Aida. 'I come from the town, you see.'

'From a big town?'

'From Tuz,' said Aida. There was an uncomfortable silence.

'Was there a high school there?'

'In Tuz? Yes, I lived just beside it. That was handy, but I was always late.'

Antonia laughed. 'Yes, the pupils I had to tell off most for lateness lived next door to the school.'

'What, here?' asked Aida.

'No, in a town the same size as your Tuz, east of Sarajevo. I was the headmistress. I moved after I married.' She beckoned Aida and walked ahead of her to a little cemetery. It was hot on the hillside. The only movement in the close afternoon air was the vibration of the crickets vigorously rubbing their wings together.

Aida looked around, embarrassed. She saw Catholic and Serbian Orthodox crosses, and pillars topped with stone turbans where Muslims were buried. All the different tombstones were placed next to each other at random, though in orderly rows. The symmetry of the graveyard, with its straight paths and tombstones, contrasted sharply with the chaos of the village below.

'Why is it that they can be neighbours here,' said Antonia, sighing, 'and not down there?' She stopped at a simple grave on which fresh wild flowers lay. Aida read the text, carved in wood: 'Jovo Rodić, 1940–1993, special feature: human'. She turned a surprised face to Antonia.

'That's what he wanted,' said Antonia, arranging the flowers. She gazed at the date. Jovo was a war child, born in the same year as herself, when Yugoslavia came into the war against Germany and Italy, but still more against itself. Violent battles had broken out between Communists and Nationalists in the country. She thought of her father, who had fought on the side of the partisans, the Yugoslav Communists. When the Nazis were beaten and her father came home he had hung a huge portrait above the chimney-piece. For years Antonia had not known who it was that gazed so sternly down at them and of whom her father spoke with such profound emotion. Later he had explained that this was Josip Broz Tito, leader of the partisans and now of all Yugoslavia. Tito would make the country strong, he explained to Antonia, because Tito had not only defeated the Nazis but also the Slav rabble, the Chetniks and the Ustasha, who were not one whit better.

Her father was a convinced Communist, who to the distress of his wife had turned his back on the Church. This sometimes led to quarrels which ended in bitter silence. Her mother took the majestic portrait off the nail to hang up a crucifix, and her father changed them back again. They never even considered the compromise of a second nail. Antonia was startled when she heard Aida cough behind her. She even blushed a little, because the girl must be thinking she was mourning for her husband. Awkwardly she tried to pick up the thread of their conversation.

'Aida, you come from Tuz. Have you any family still living there?'

'No,' said Aida, 'we all had to leave. There was a convoy to the coast, they said. So we left Tuz together, my mother and I.'

'Aida is a Muslim name. Are you a Mohammedan?'

'No, an atheist,' said Aida. She looked out of the corner of her eye at the woman she might now have offended, but Antonia smiled. 'My father was an atheist, too.'

Intuitively they realized that they need not go on talking. Each had told the other something about herself, and from now on they could simply chat.

When they went into the kitchen Napoleon was asleep. He did not even raise his head. Only his nose twitched, then he went on with his dream, reassured.

Antonia was worried about her stores of 'dry goods', as she called the packets of sugar, rice, coffee and baking powder. Fat, too, was running out. She should have been receiving new supplies today at latest, but no one had come.

Aida watched as she inspected her cupboards and counted packets and tins, talking quietly to herself.

'Do you really get help from the Blues? How do they know you're here? On my way I never saw them stop at villages like this one, they raced past like bullets. Driving fast, that's something they're good at…'

Aida jumped as Antonia turned on her abruptly.

She folded her freckled arms and leaned against the sink. 'Don't you trust me, is that it?'

Aida bowed her head in silence.

'So it's no,' said Antonia, 'at least, not enough. All over the world there are angels and villains, my girl. I happen to know two angels, whom I gratefully allow to help me. One is a doctor, the other a soldier, and they know my situation. Before tomorrow I was to have got dry goods and oil and batteries and soap, from people moving inwards across the country. But they have not come. That is a bad sign, Aida. It indicates blockades, perhaps fighting. Let's go to bed early. Don't be frightened if Napoleon starts barking. Stay lying quietly behind the partition in the hidden room. And don't be frightened if you hear strange voices. Or hear me laughing, for instance. Don't look. Remember that it's play-acting. That's how it has to be, there's no other way.'

'But who is coming?' asked Aida.

'Trash,' said Antonia. 'And perhaps they won't come, after all.'

# Chapter 4

Aida lay there for hours, her eyes wide open, staring into the darkness. The thunder of the storm in the mountains sounded like gunfire, and every time the old dog howled in the house she started up. But apart from the storm and Napoleon talking in his sleep, nothing at all happened. That made her quite cross when she got dressed in the morning and went to the kitchen.

'Ha,' said Antonia dully, but without turning round. She spread biscuits with the last of the crumbling cheese, and Aida could see from her attitude that she too had slept badly. In silence they sat down at the table. Aida poured little dry crumbs from her right hand into the palm of her left, looking up from time to time and catching Antonia's brooding, prematurely-aged expression. She looked more than ever like a farmer and less like the headmistress of a girls' high school. Where were her bookshelves, desk and writing things, where were the clothes she had worn then, the brooches, the nail files? Here, under the rubble? Aida tried to imagine Antonia in a school hall or working at a desk, but the cotton apron, unkempt hair and calloused hands stopped her imagination dead. Only when she spoke could Aida hear the literally buried past in her voice and recognize that Antonia was something other than she seemed.

If only she would talk a little, it would help! But Antonia was silent and depressed, and the later it grew, the more openly she showed it. Again and again she went out to the terrace to stare up at the Gora, or down the dusty, deserted road which ran through Brodište to the mountains. 'Where on earth are they?'

No one came. No soldiers with kalashnikovs, no angel with food parcels, not even her nephew with fresh water. 'What are they up to?' Her anxiety infected Napoleon, who stumbled in and out of the kitchen, until she put him on his lead for fear that he might escape to the stream in an unguarded moment. The dog was thirsty, but there was no water left.

'Isn't there a well or a pool where I could get some water?' asked Aida. She wanted to get away, out of the house. Both the dog and the woman were getting on her nerves.

'There is a spring, but you have to know the way there.'

'Explain it to me and I'll go.'

'No, I would have to show you, but I can't leave. I must stay here, in case they come.'

'It's already nearly four o'clock.' Aida looked up at the sun. 'Half-past four,' said Antonia, with an amused chuckle.

It was the first time she had laughed. 'Aida, I'll make a suggestion. I will go to the spring and you stay here. You need not be afraid of Josip, he will look more flabbergasted than you. So you don't need to watch the mountain, but do keep an eye on the road. And whether they are good or bad people, Napoleon will bark! So they can't take you by surprise. You will have time to hide, and I shall hear Napoleon.'

'And then?' asked Aida anxiously. 'The door is open, the dog is lying here, you have gone. They will search.'

Antonia opened a kitchen cupboard and set a bottle and three glasses on the table. 'No, they will drink. And I...' she studied the contents and tipped the slivovitz to

32

and fro. 'I shall be back before that's finished.'

As soon as Antonia had gone Aida went to sit in a square higher up in the village, from which she could observe the road. She was sweating, felt miserable and dirty, and morbidly suspicious where Antonia was concerned. Again and again she looked round at the mountain, because, after all, the boys existed! But what about the cars? She turned back to the road, where nothing had passed for four days. Where was the clandestine traffic she had been hearing about? Where were the people who supplied Brodište and might give her a lift? Could Antonia have made it all up, just to keep Aida with her? But then where did the coffee and cheese and other luxuries come from? Aida had a sudden idea: they had not come overland but from the hold of an aircraft! Last winter food had been dropped, the bales sometimes falling on the heads of refugees, sometimes sinking into the snow in deserted areas. Suddenly she laughed, and stood up. To hell with the wretched road! She slapped the sand and dust from her clothes and returned to the kitchen. Napoleon wagged his tail and came to meet her. Aida could hear his claws scratching on the tiles until the lead was too taut and throttled his bark. He looked pleadingly at her: he was thirsty, but there was nothing but plum brandy. The green bottle stood untouched on the kitchen table. Aida was thirsty, too.

She was sleeping curled up between wall and table when Antonia returned. She raised her eyebrows, but was too busy with the dog. 'Quiet, boy, be quiet!' She unscrewed the jerry can and, as usual, filled the dog's bowl first. After

33

that she poured water into a kettle on the stove. Aida had woken up and was looking on drowsily. She heard Napoleon lapping, saw the flames crackling in the stove, heard the scrape of a wooden spoon, with which Antonia was stirring something in a saucepan – homely, peaceful sounds, which told her she could sleep on where she was.

'You really are a one!' Antonia shook her head. 'A quarter litre, I should say. Was it nice?'

Aida struggled up. Her shoulder hurt from the way she had been lying but otherwise there was nothing wrong.

'Home-made, Jovo's recipe. Was it good?'

'Yes. Sorry.'

'Fine. It would have done him good to hear that.' Suppressing a smile, Antonia tipped a tin of beans into the saucepan. 'I'm making...well, what am I making? Soup, I'll just call it soup. The water from the spring is cloudy and has to be boiled. I really don't understand why Josip has not come, but it may be for the best. I could not have given him anything. I've used everything up, and I shall get new supplies tomorrow. Perhaps. And then I shall have something for him too.'

Aida nodded. To her alcohol-clouded brain it did not matter if she was hearing truth or lies. Even when Antonia said that they would go to bed early again, she remained remarkably calm. 'Not a sound, understand?' said the old woman. 'No matter who or what you hear, you just stay where you are. No one looks behind the partition.'

After going outside for a moment, Aida returned to her room. The crooked walls no longer worried her, especially as the kitchen was no longer straight either.

34

She undressed slowly. She had never drunk alcohol before, just a little wine, a little beer, but never slivovitz or raki. Giggling, she searched for the neck opening in Antonia's nightdress.

*'Get in!' yelled the man beside the bus. He looked at his watch and drove the women who were trying to get on more and more roughly. 'Hurry, you Turks, hurry!'*

*Beside him stood a dog, barking in imitation of his orders. 'Quickly, we're expected, their stock of dry goods is finished!' Aida was one of the last to get on the coach. Behind a steamed-up window she could make out her mother's face. 'Hey, Miss, not you!' shouted the man. 'You've been drinking, I can smell it!' He caught her roughly by the arm and pulled her off the step. 'Turn on the light! Why is there no light in here? Dragan, get the torch from the car!'*

Aida lay motionless, listening to the voices in her dream and in the kitchen. She was in that stage of sleep when dream and reality merge.

'Dragan, get the torch from the car!'

That sentence again. She stared at the wooden partition wall, behind which there was a scraping of chair legs, barking and footsteps. The events of the dream vanished and only the kitchen was left. Slowly it dawned on her that they had arrived, 'the trash', as Antonia called them. A shudder, first only at the top of her spine, spread through her whole body until her teeth were almost chattering. She hugged her arms round her shoulders and had great difficulty in not screaming aloud.

About half-way up the north face of the Gora, Josip and Haris were quarrelling. Josip wanted to go down, Haris was trying to persuade him to stay at all costs. 'They'll catch you, boy,' he prophesied. 'As soon as you set foot in the kitchen they'll beat you up.'

'They can't see from my face that I'm a Croat, can they?'

'So what, they can use a young Chetnik too. Anything that has two hands and can shoot they'll take along with them.'

Josip clenched his fists. 'We left too late. If we had left an hour earlier we would now...'

'Be lying tied up on the floor.'

'Get lost!'

'But it's true,' said Haris. 'Let's say we had arrived at your aunt's an hour ago. She would have got out of bed, lit the lamp and made coffee. We talk about the girl. She denies everything. A knocking at the door. Open up! And then? Would we have jumped the men? No! Your aunt would have ordered us straight behind the partition wall, where of course the girl sleeps.

'You and I introduce ourselves briefly. Don't be afraid, we're good guys. She doesn't hear. She's terrified. Next door the men come into the kitchen and closer still, until two idiots are standing, invisibly, beside her bed. She...'

Josip interrupted him. 'Shut up – you're right. An hour earlier would not have helped. But what do we do now?'

Silently they leaned forward and looked down on the dark village of Brodište, where a light was burning in only one house. The jerry can stood between them. They had wanted to make the descent by daylight, but problems with Mila and Ramiz had held them up.

36

When they set out it was already dark. Josip had wavered, preferring to put off the visit, but Haris wanted to go. It was often like that. In their friendship they were like sun and moon, complementing each other wonderfully, but never able to agree, always arguing about time and place. Josip felt that he was the moon, the one who reflected the other's light, sometimes quite literally.

For as long as they could remember they had lived next door to each other in the centre of Sarajevo. But Josip had always been just a little bit less skilful, quick and intelligent than his neighbour. Not that Haris had ever exploited it. The problem was rather that it made Josip suffer. Whether it was a matter of 'grown-up' teeth, chest hair or exams, Haris was ahead of him in everything. He had extraordinary parents, too. His father was a professor and presenter of arts programmes, his mother an actress. Although their home on the other side of the staircase entrance was the same as Josip's flat, it smelled and looked different, elegant and mysterious, with heavy velour curtains, paintings and books. You could breathe the air of theatres and studios there. Sometimes Josip had been envious, then proud of such comments as 'Hey, Josip, you're Haris's friend, aren't you?' Or 'Do you go to Musanović's house – you know, the television man?' So he had become the moon.

But Haris would not even let him reign over the night. Instead of going to sleep they had clambered down the steep, dark path. 'Right now?' Ramiz and Mila asked in astonishment. 'Yes, right now, thanks to you!' Haris had snarled at them. 'No water down there, no rice up here. Sleep well!'

And off they went, leaving Ramiz and Mila behind on the mountain. They were half-way down when Josip saw the car. 'Haris, they're back. Look!' Squatting on the path they watched the car: an army jeep, turning into the village with its headlights full on. 'Oh God,' murmured Haris. 'Oh God!'

The roles had changed. Now it was Josip who wanted to go on and Haris who preferred to wait. 'Trust Antonia, Josip. It's not their first visit. She knows what to do.'

'What about the girl?' said Josip.

Haris had no answer to that. The girl, he had to admit, was an uncertain factor.

'She'll think of something, she'll find a way,' he reassured Josip. 'She's smart, that aunt of yours.'

Both of them were remembering the time when they themselves had lived in the village, but while Haris's clearest memory was of Antonia's quick-wittedness, Josip concentrated on her weakest moments.

He knew about the supply of slivovitz under the kitchen floor. That was her laughing gas and tear gas in this war of nerves – her weapon, that turned blustering men into mumbling drunks. He knew how she did it, too. Again and again Haris and he had been silent witnesses, sweating behind the partition wall. As soon as soldiers arrived his aunt would hide them, and chatter away like some foolish female to her visitors. Sometimes she was Jelena, sometimes Greta, now Orthodox, now Catholic, then Communist again. And when in doubt, neutral. Like a chameleon, she adapted to the men, who came more and more often, either suspicious of the woman in the half-ruined house, or looking for a cup of coffee and a taste of home life, or a swig of slivovitz. There were decent men among them, but the majority were riff-raff. They bullied and humiliated her, and when Josip heard her hysterical laughter at such times he was afraid, because Antonia was balancing on the brink of the unbearable. He would drive his nails into his palms and ached to charge into the kitchen and kick the men.

That was why Haris and he had set up camp on the mountain; it was getting too dangerous down in the village. But whenever he went back with water he reproached himself. He should have fetched her as soon as they had found somewhere to live on the Gora. She had gone mad with loneliness before he and Haris came, and now she was alone again. Seven weeks had passed since then, with one interruption, when Mila and Ramiz spent the night at her house. Josip thought about the girl. On the one hand her coming might help his aunt, on the other hand it was a new burden among so many. If not from loneliness, she might go mad from nervous exhaustion.

'I'm going,' he said, standing up.

'Where?' asked Haris, taken aback.

Josip smiled, feeling himself suddenly the stronger. 'Not back up there, wimp. The other way, down there!' He picked up the heavy can in which the mountain water slopped about, and walked on down without paying any attention to his friend.

'What are you going to do?' asked Haris.

'Take the water, as usual.'

Haris switched on the pocket torch and glanced quickly at his watch. 'Hm, fifty minutes.'

'What?'

39

'They've been in there for fifty minutes.'

'That's eight to ten glasses.'

'Don't forget the driver,' said Haris.

'Okay, he only drinks half as much, but he's not sober by now, either.'

Haris rolled up his sleeves. 'Right, this is going to be a pushover. We'll polish off two each.'

They looked at each other, laughing. Naturally they were not going to do any fighting. The men were at their worst when they had been drinking. They might be more likely to fall over but also quicker to draw a gun.

'Here, give me the water,' said Haris. 'You'll be getting a crippled arm.'

Josip gave him the can. 'Walk right behind me. There are great holes in the path here and it's dangerous to use the torch.'

Although he knew the path backwards, and better than Haris, Josip slowed down. 'A stone,' he whispered over his shoulder. 'Tree trunk. Hole.'

They were now so close to Brodište that they could see the outlines of the first ruins. As if by agreement they stopped. Haris puffed and put down the jerry can. 'Shall we wait here?'

'Yes,' whispered Josip. 'They must be leaving at any minute.' Unless something terrible had happened, but he dared not think about that. Beside him Haris was drumming on his teeth with his fingers.

At last they heard a door opening and a man's voice singing. A second voice joined in. Someone laughed. Someone cursed. *Jedan peva, drugi svira!* bawled the drunken singers. The engine of the jeep started with a loud squealing noise: the driver was drunk, too. The vehicle wobbled over the rubble, out of the village, and disappeared into the night with its four occupants. Josip put his fingers to his lips and whistled: high, low, high, low. They listened tensely.

'Nothing,' said Haris. 'Funny. Try again.'

This time they heard a faint bark. They walked to the little square, where Josip repeated the signal. The dog barked again and suddenly the kitchen door opened just a crack. 'Josip?' they heard Antonia's mortally weary voice. 'Josip…Josha, is that you?'

Josip rushed to his favourite aunt, who only came up to his chest, and hugged her to him. 'You must get away from here! It can't go on like this!'

She patted him on the back. 'Calm down, my boy, calm down. They got drunk, that's all. Hallo, Haris, you there too? Come in.' The kitchen was so thick with smoke that the outlines of all the objects were blurred and their vocal chords were affected. The boys stared in silence at the table, covered with dirty glasses, cigarette butts and scraps of food. Napoleon lay exhausted and panting in a corner. 'Is he ill?' asked Josip.

'Not really. They poured raki into his drinking bowl, the fools. It will pass.' With a surge of energy Antonia tore open the kitchen door. She too was having problems with the pungent air. 'Well, Josip, give me some water. I don't feel very well.' She sat down and put her head in her hands. 'Why have you come so late?'

'It was to do with Mila and Ramiz,' said Josip, looking for a clean glass among all the mess. From time to time he glanced at the passage with the partition wall, and then across at his friend.

41

'Antonia,' said Haris, after she had drunk, 'have you got a young girl in the house?'

Her head came up with a start.

'I saw her,' said Josip. 'The day before yesterday. She must go, and you too, Aunt! It can't go on like this!' He nodded his head at the table and the empty bottles beside it.

His aunt stood up. 'Her name is Aida and she's not a child. I'll go and ask her what she wants to do. All right?' Tired as she was, she ordered the two boys to stay in the kitchen while she moved the partition.

'Aida?'

The room looked empty. Antonia fetched the torch from the kitchen and found the girl stretched full-length on the floor between the wall and the bed. When Antonia touched her, she screamed.

# Chapter 5

The sun had come back! Antonia had put Aida in a chair on the little square, where she slowly calmed down again. She felt her cheeks glowing, but after that horrible night she could not have enough of the heat. Brodište was a trap into which she had automatically fallen at the sight of an orchard. How was she ever to get away from here? She could have gone with the boys, who had climbed back up the Gora at first light. She had glanced quickly at them and shaken her head: she would stay here. At least for the time being, until she was strong and fit enough to set out again.

Feeling hot, she went to the kitchen for a glass of water and rolled it across her burning cheeks before drinking from it. The icon still hung above the kitchen table. A long-nosed saint with almond-shaped eyes was blessing a peasant woman.

'Oh yes, I must move that,' she heard Antonia comment. Josip's aunt had gone to look down the road for the umpteenth time, and came panting in again.

'Why an icon?' asked Aida. 'How did you know they were Chetniks?'

Antonia laughed. 'Have you ever seen how soldiers mark the front line with little flags on a map? I have a map like that in my head. Recently Brodište seems to be Serbian again; before that it was Croatian. It's disputed territory that they claim in turn, as if they were playing ball. Hey, you're sunburnt.'

'Why do you stay here?'

'To help the boys, of course! I was in luck in May when they moved the approach route for supplies over a mountain ridge, so that transports came through the village. They have helped me four times. Spanish Blue Helmets and a Danish doctor. If they don't come now it's something to do with those fighters.'

'The Chetniks?' asked Aida.

'Or some other trash. Perhaps you should decide to go up the mountain, after all. There is another girl there, Mila. I sent her and her friend up.' Antonia sighed. 'Like Peter at heaven's gate,' she added softly. 'It would only be for a short time, they said. All four of them planned to go on to the coast, but it's cool and pleasant up there. They keep on putting off their departure.'

Involuntarily Aida looked up at the huge mountain. She could not imagine how the others could live there. 'Have they built themselves huts?'

'There is a little chapel up there, by an old cemetery, I think. Haris knows all about it. He discovered something on the southern slopes of the Gora and has been driving Josip half mad with it. It's no good asking me, I've never been up there. Some peculiarities of an area or a village you only discover when you're young; otherwise you never see them. When Jovo and I came here we were already over forty. We didn't know this part of Bosnia, but Jovo was able to open a practice here. Iron ore had been found in the area, a mine was dug, workers came, lower and senior management came, and the newcomers wanted a dentist. Really it was a filthy hole where fifty per cent of the people had something to do with iron ore. It took me a long time to get used to it.'

'Were you sorry to have moved here?'

Antonia shook her head. She had had no regrets, though she had really intended to remain single. She had been in love a few times, but never deeply enough to get married. Her pupils came first. About fourteen years ago doubts had crept in. Was teaching really her only fulfilment in life? And still more important: did it help? Was she capable of dissuading young people from the narrow nationalism that led nowhere and constantly ruined everything? She sensed that it was all boiling up again in Serbia. Tito was dead, and neo-nationalists saw their chances clear. Her pupils sang satirical songs about the 'Balijas', their contemptuous nickname for Muslims. And gypsies were known as 'blacks'. So what had become of the famous equality of all peoples?

'No,' she said aloud. 'No, I never regretted moving to Brodište. I had been teaching for sixteen years when I met Jovo. He was a good man, and the only dentist I was not afraid of.'

Aida turned away from the window and looked across to the hall where the ruin began. With Antonia's books, exercise books and writing things were a large dentist's chair and horrible instruments. Why was Antonia talking more and more about herself? It was becoming more difficult all the time not to respond.

'Oh, Tuz was a hole too.'

'Yes, but Tuz has character! The town has a soul in the centre, with its shiny mosaics and its beautiful fountain.'

A cracked soul, thought Aida, because all the minarets had been snapped off like flowers and all the mosques blown up, and not so very long ago. Before that, Tuz had been flooded with thousands of refugees from the surrounding villages. Being believers, they visited the mosques and converted Tuz into a pious town again overnight. After that, Mujaheddin, Iranians and Pakistanis camped in the barracks. No one was interested in them and their holy war, and yet the atmosphere changed. Changed again, in fact. Priests spoke on television, and in the advertisements companies congratulated each other on Ramadan. The old town seemed to become more and more conscious of its Muslim past. Khojas, more obsessed than ever, called the faithful to prayer, and people who had seldom prayed before now came to kneel and celebrate the month of fasting once again. Among them were some of Aida's friends, not as obsessed as the Mujaheddin, whom they secretly still feared, but convinced of the need for an identity. Were they called Muslims? Good, they would be Muslims! That was the strange thing about this war. It radicalized people. Once Tuz had been a town with a Muslim majority, who did little about it, then it had become a threatened town full of persecuted Muslims, then a bulwark of piety, and then it was destroyed.

'Tuz is in ruins,' she said bitterly. 'You would scarcely recognize it.'

'Really?' asked Antonia, horrified. 'Even the fountain in the market-place, and the white mosque?'

Aida nodded. Everything that recalled the five hundred years of Turkish rule had been destroyed by the Chetniks. It had made her furious! Even as a child she could not bear it if a drawing was torn or a hut kicked down, and she was the same today. She looked at the icon with its super-sentimental, long-nosed, long-necked saint. She would never lay a finger on it!

'Aida,' said Antonia, 'you did say you had left Tuz with your mother. Where is she now – your mother?'

Although Aida had been expecting the question, she

took fright when it came. She didn't want to talk about it here.

'Where is she?'

But Aida shrugged her shoulders, closing up like a clam.

At that moment Napoleon joined in. Recovering from the raki, he started barking as hard as he could. 'Oh, the boys!' said Antonia. 'Have they come at last?' Pulling a comb through her hair she hurried excitedly out to the kitchen.

White UN vehicles were standing in the road, and hanging half out of one of them was a man who waved exuberantly.

'Pedro!' cried Antonia, making a painful effort to run as fast as possible over the rubble. The dog, old as he was, ran faster, but he had four legs to keep his balance.

Laughing, Antonia gripped the outstretched hands of the man who had jumped out of his jeep. He was short and agile, with a princely moustache and a bald, sunburnt head.

'Antonia, little mother, how are you?'

'You've come just in time, angel! I have nothing left, not even rice.'

'Then we'll do something about that right away.' Pedro told the driver of one vehicle to unload the boxes he had set aside. The tarpaulin was hastily unhooked from the cargo space.

'We shall have to be quick,' he said. 'We're sitting here like a long white target in the valley.

'I haven't heard a shot for weeks.'

'I have,' he replied laconically, pointing to the bullet holes in the coachwork.

The five of them went into the house, followed by the dog, too unhinged with joy to know whose calves to snap at first.

'And how are the children?' asked Pedro. He knew her from the days when the boys were still living with her. In fact it was they who had begged him to stop one afternoon. They had appeared like ghosts from the shattered village and had jumped into the road in front of his convoy, shouting and waving wildly. The old woman had been ill then. The next time he came through Brodište she was already a little better, and the third time he had noticed that Antonia had taken charge of the boys. From then on he called her 'little mother', which she obviously enjoyed. The fourth time a surprise awaited him: the boys had gone and in their place he met a girl and her boyfriend.

'Ramon, wasn't it?'

'Ramiz.'

'Has his hand healed a little?'

'He still complains of pain. I'm afraid the wound is inflamed.'

'No!' Pedro stopped. 'Hjalte, the doctor, isn't with us, but I have got a medical orderly.'

'Fine,' said Antonia, 'but he certainly won't want to go up to the Gora. Ramiz and Mila don't live here any more. Now I have four up on the mountain and a new one in the house, a girl.'

'Really?' asked Pedro incredulously. Sweat was streaming under his shirt, over which he wore a bullet-proof vest. It was no fun keeping his balance on the rubble with the heavy vest and a case. 'Get off!' he snarled at Napoleon.

'Oh, he's happy, he's only playing, he won't bite you, angel!'

'Yes, yes,' said Pedro.

Silently he and the other men dragged the boxes into the kitchen. Antonia glanced into the hall and behind the partition wall. What had happened to Aida? 'Water?' she offered, and then, with a wink, 'Strong water?'

Pedro, who had been speaking French with her, consulted the others in Spanish. All three shook their sweaty heads. They wanted to go on as quickly as possible.

'They are frightened,' said Pedro. 'It's a bit tricky here, little mother! Why don't you and the children leave here and go to the coast? You will have to do it in the end anyway, because they wouldn't last a week up there in winter. Talk to them, persuade them! Perhaps I can organize a lift. Where is the girl?'

'I don't know,' said Antonia. 'She was in the kitchen just now, but she's pretty nervous. I worry about her. She must be the first to get away! Pedro, when could she go with you? When are you driving south again?'

The others were getting impatient, and making it obvious by scratching their necks, clearing their throats, or scraping their feet like restless horses.

*'No te preocupes, hombre!'* cried Pedro. 'In six days, I should think. I can't be more precise than that. We are on our way to Mudrovac, a besieged Muslim enclave, but the question is whether we get there… *Siiii, paciencia!* It's just like a toll road. Every stop means that we lose part of our load to the local fighters! They run around, rosy and well-fed, while the people die in misery. Do you know our latest nickname? SERBOFOR, they call us, as if we were working for Serbia! But I must make it in six days. If it takes any longer, you will know why.' The Spaniard leaned forward to give her two kisses. 'Keep it

up, little mother! Adios!' Then he left, his grumbling men at his heels.

Antonia watched him go, feeling depressed. She had been looking forward to a chat about Pedro's family, the situation in Split, newspaper headlines, the course of the war, Europe, public opinion. What did she know, sitting here now? Her world had shrunk. The only news that reached her came from the barrel of a gun. 'Adios then,' she said quietly, brushing a tear from her nose. All the trucks started up again. Sunk in thought, she watched the elongated cloud of dust in which the convoy crawled up the next mountain. Sensing her mood, Napoleon put his head on her lap. She stroked the dog, gave him water and felt the boxes standing in the middle of the kitchen. 'Aida!' she called into the stillness. 'Aida?' The girl would help her to stow the supplies.

When no answer came Antonia grew worried. Could the child have run away? She obeyed an instinct and went into the little rom, but the girl was not there, even in the narrow space between bed and wall.

'Aida!' she called outside, urging the dog on. 'Seek, Napoleon, seek!' With him she clambered over the rubble in the roads and lanes, constantly making a funnel of her hands and shouting, 'Aida, come back! They've gone!'

Suddenly they saw the girl, standing so close to them that they were quite startled, and looking at them suspiciously. Napoleon wagged his tail.

'Are you coming home with us?' asked Antonia. 'I've got a mountain of supplies.'

The innocent question did wonders: Aida nodded and walked off with them. Antonia sighed with relief and Napoleon licked her hand.

# Chapter 6

Mila skilfully cut open the skinned rabbit and whipped out the entrails with a few swift movements. When she heard Josip and Haris making vomiting noises she laughed. 'You town boys can't do anything, can you? All you see is neatly packed chunks of animals in the supermarket and you forget that they once had legs and a head as well.'

'It's worse than that,' said Josip. 'Sometimes we saw nothing at all in the supermarket. We've almost forgotten what meat looks like. Isn't that right, Haris? The price stayed the same, seventy marks per kilo, but you couldn't get it.'

'What did you eat, then?' asked Mila.

'Cheese pitta without cheese,' said Josip, 'rice pitta or rice schnitzels, rice with tomato sauce, flour soup, soya schnitzels, stinging nettle soufflé…'

'Or nothing,' Haris added, watching Mila spitting the rabbit and placing the metal rod across the forks of two twigs pushed into the ground. She looked critically at the fire, smouldering golden-orange, and crawled over to one of the twigs to turn the spit. And so the skinned and disembowelled rabbit began a pirouette which was to end in their stomachs. In his too? In town he had been a vegetarian like his father and mother and hundreds of thousands of involuntary supporters. But here, just here, it was difficult. Fruit, nuts and mushrooms alone were not enough. He was sometimes perishing with hunger, but had still resisted when Mila laid her traps. He jumped when the girl stopped turning the spit. For him the animal was ready much too soon — and what was there on it, anyway? Four meagre portions.

Josip saw him hesitate and gave him a nudge. 'Go on, eat it!'

Haris obeyed and took his share, almost as if he were sacrificing himself, but wasn't the wretched rabbit delicious!

'Listen, Mila,' he said, blushing. 'The other traps…'

'Nothing there yet,' she said apologetically.

'Oh.' He was expecting the others to tease him, but Josip, Mila and Ramiz simply smiled.

Mila picked up the plate, the knife and the hot spit. 'No washing up, great,' she said. 'At home there were always huge stacks that my mother and I had to get through while my brothers and my father went off for a walk. Good for the digestion. They weren't interested in what was happening to our insides. Coming to the water with me, Ramiz?'

The boy stood up silently and they walked together to the foaming stream where they also filled the plastic jerry cans for Antonia. Mila chattered, Ramiz was silent.

'She talks too much,' said Haris.

'He talks too little,' said Josip.

'But she can't make up for that by talking for two.'

'She means well,' said Josip.

'Yes, but he's getting quieter and quieter.'

And then came the teasing, after all. 'The rabbit was delicious, eh, Haris?'

'Hmm, yes,' said Haris, and held his tongue about Mila.

While they were talking the boys had reached the old cemetery, where Haris spent hours every day with a small file, a brush, pencil and paper.

'I've found a fantastic stone now!' he said, with a light in his eyes that Josip recognized from his father, the famous Professor Musanovic.

'What sort of stone?' asked Josip. 'Flat on the ground, or a standing square, tall and tapering, a pillar, a cross or a little house?'

The irony of his recital completely escaped Haris.

'House-shaped,' he said. 'With images, man, so perfect!' Haris spread out his arms as if to embrace the entire field on the mountainside, where dozens of light grey stones, all lined up in an east-west direction, adorned the slopes of the Gora. 'If my father knew about this stone, he would come and get it personally.'

'Why?'

'For his museum! A monster, I tell you. About twelve tons, I should think.'

'And you want to take that through the check points to Sarajevo?'

'No, not now of course,' said Haris irritably. 'The Serbs would think it was a plastic bomb. But in normal circumstances my father would come and get it.'

Why, thought Josip, did the stone have to be in a museum? You could find stones like that all over Bosnia. Sometimes on their own, sometimes in small groups, sometimes in large numbers, as on the Gora. The people called them *Stara Groblja*, or more simply, *stećci*. No one was quite sure if they were monuments or if the corpses of heretics were really buried there. From time to time scholars had dug up parts of skeletons; it was the exception, but happened often enough to frighten people. Mila, for instance, who could skin and disembowel a rabbit without batting an eyelid, would have nothing to do with the *stećci*. She did not like to admit it, but she always made excuses when Haris came and called her because he had found something new. And yet she attached as much importance to the graves as the boys. They were as much part of the landscape as the name Bosnia itself.

'Why does it have to be in a museum?' asked Josip.

'The stone? To save it. If it stays here the process of weathering by wind and rain will continue. Or another madman will come, a bridge or road-builder who wants convenient, ready-cut blocks which only need the sculpture planed off. Do you know how many *stećci* the Austrians took last century…'

'Yes, I know, you've told me,' said Josip. 'Don't tell me everything twice. Just show me the new stone.'

Haris's face brightened.

He zigzagged through the graves to a stone in the shape of a little house. 'No, don't look yet,' he said, like a child who has practically finished a drawing, but still wants to change something. He quickly took the little brush from his breast pocket and dusted it over the decorative areas. 'Now!' Josip turned. It really was a splendid stone, with a number of unusual images on all four sides.

'Do you recognize the luminous cross?' asked Haris. His fingers stroked the relief.

'Yes, I can see it.'

'Do you see, the cross moves into a sun wheel, both upwards and sideways.'

'Yes, I see that.' Josip also saw that the cross branched off in circular spirals. It symbolized life and was utterly

54

different from the crucifixes he knew, with the suffering body of Jesus.

'And just have a look at the long side!' said the elated Haris.

Josip walked round the *stećak* with him and saw a hunting scene: a stag, pursued by two horsemen, and a patch which might possibly be a dog.

'What's that round thing there?' he asked, pointing to an unusual circle above the broad antlers.

'A crown, a sun or a halo,' said Haris. 'I don't know exactly, either, but I can explain the deer to you. The deer is the symbol of the baptized, spiritually reborn human being, but on this stone it also symbolizes persecution. The people who hid on the Gora were being persecuted, hunted, do you see? Come on, there's something interesting on the next side, too.'

Haris was impatient and irritated by Josip, who sat without moving.

'Listen,' said Josip, 'detonations.'

'What?'

'Shells, rockets, mines!'

Haris came back, nonplussed. 'Damn it, you're right.'

Together they listened to the thunder noise that had become so familiar after years of siege. But in fact it sounded less dangerous than elsewhere in the space and breadth of the Gora.

'Where can it be?' asked Haris.

Josip shrugged. What was there to be shot at, in an area where everything man-made was already in ruins? Nothing, he reasoned logically. But what was the use of reason in a country where logic had gone missing? Even the village that existed only thanks to one last inhabitant could suddenly become strategically important. In fact it already was, because the area was contested by Serbs and Croats. Josip began to sweat. If armies would smash up an undamaged town to get it in their power, they would just as readily smash up a town that was already in ruins. Perhaps even more readily. That was the logic of war. He should never have left Antonia down there.

'Where are you going?' asked Haris.

'To the lookout!' With Haris close behind him, Josip rushed up from the cemetery to the highest point of the mountain. The Gora was almost bare there, with only a few sparse bushes and tussocks and boulders split by rock-falls. Shreds of cloud often drifted round the stony plateau, but today it was clear. On days like this one could see for many kilometres, especially to the west.

'Well?' asked Haris eagerly. 'Shall I get the telescope?'

Josip hesitated. Far away, down there on the northern flank, lay Brodište. 'Can you see anything?' he asked.

'No plumes of smoke, if that's what you mean. They're busy somewhere else.'

'I'm going down!' said Josip. 'I'm going to fetch her, Haris. If necessary, I'll carry her!'

'Your aunt? On the Gora?' asked Mila, her eyes wide with astonishment, the dark irises swimming in the white. She put her hands on her hips and looked meaningly upwards.

'Why not?' asked Ramiz, and these words, from someone who never spoke, were what carried weight. The three of them looked at her.

'Yes, why not?' said Josip. 'It means we can stop hauling water, and the goat will have a great time, too."

'What about the rice, and the tins?' asked Mila.

'Well, now we've got your rabbits,' said Josip. He was getting annoyed with Mila. 'I won't have my aunt left in misery so that you can have your sardines! And in any case, the Blues aren't coming again! We can see that by now. All she's got left are her vegetables, the goat, and a supply of slivovitz. I'm going to get her out of there, Mila!'

'And the girl?' asked Mila, because after their last visit Haris and Josip had told her about Aida.

'What do you mean, "and the girl"?'

'Is she coming here too?' asked Mila.

Sighing, Josip listened to the rushing water. They were sitting in their favourite place in the alder brake by the stream, where you could not hear the shells exploding down below. Haris had seen through the telescope that Izvor was being bombarded. They were all shocked, because Izvor was a beautiful, old place built in terraces against the mountainside.

'It's up to her,' said Josip.

'So it could happen?' asked Mila.

'Or not, all according.'

It was too much for Haris. 'Stop it!' he cried. 'Let's fill the jerry cans and go down. They're dying of thirst, they're drying out! If they want us to, we'll evacuate the whole village up here: the goat, the dog, and the people. And if they want to stay, at least they'll have water. It's no use rabbiting on about what 'perhaps', 'in that case', 'may be' or 'nevertheless' could happen. But you can't force them either, Josip. Your aunt won't be forced to do anything.'

Mila smiled ironically.

'She is just as self-willed and stubborn as Mila,' said Haris.

This time it was Ramiz who smiled.

Chapter 7

Antonia had rolled herself a cigarette and was sitting comfortably by the table reading the paper when the shooting began.

'Oh no,' she said, disappointed, and stopped reading. Napoleon, who had been sleeping in the shadow of the table, had jumped up and was tugging fiercely at his lead. She had tied him up when the water was finished. Luckily Josip was coming, if he dared to now.

'Where is it coming from?' asked Aida.

'Perhaps from Brezik,' said Antonia, 'or Turovi or Izvor.'

It was difficult to be sure, because the banging and rattling re-echoed ten times over from the mountains. The noise shut them in, which made the whole thing even more frightening. You could feel it everywhere, making the wooden table and the floor of the terrace shudder and shaking the walls, with their treacherous cracks. Aida could see the tremors.

'Don't go past the hall,' said Antonia, 'no further than the kitchen.'

'What if they come here too?'

'They won't, or not till later. I really must take care not to become their local!'

'What if they come sooner?'

'They won't,' Antonia repeated. But she did not really know. The certainty she radiated was for the benefit of the terrified girl sitting in the sun, her face turning redder and redder. Antonia did not want her to get sunburned. But no matter how many luxury articles Pedro had given her, the newspapers, tobacco and shampoo never

59

included anything for sunburn.

She tried again to pinpoint the noise and then, which was even more difficult, to put herself in the place of the trash. Probably they had stopped the convoy and partly plundered it. And probably they figured that Pedro had supplied their 'innkeeper' on his fifth tour through the village. How attractive to have a pub where not only slivovitz but also salami could be had for nothing! Antonia shifted uneasily to and fro on her chair. She had folded the newspaper.

'Don't you smoke?' she asked Aida.

Aida shook her head, and watched as Antonia lit her fourth cigarette. She held it between thumb and forefinger, her palm turned outwards, and for some reason this irritated Aida. 'Did you smoke while you were working at the school?'

'Why do you want to know that?'

Aida blushed. 'No reason.' She could not understand herself. Why was her attention caught by trivial things, when the ground and the walls were shaking?

'I smoke like a man, is that what you mean?'

'Of course not!'

'You're a bad liar, like Josip.' Antonia burst out laughing. 'Do you know what I've just been reading in this Croat paper? Tourism is beginning to revive in Istria; Florida is fighting an oil slick, and the Pope is recovering.'

Aida looked up. 'Well, and?'

'Well, that was the news I've been longing for all these months!'

Aida gave a forced laugh. She had tried to read, but the articles did not interest her. And when the shooting began there was no chance of reading an article through to the end. Her eyes flew over headlines, pictures and advertisements that meant nothing to her.

She noticed that the noise was dying down and the table was no longer shaking, but instead of relief she felt a new fear. 'Not till later,' Antonia had said, and 'later' had begun now. Aida took a drastic decision.

'Why are you looking at me like that?' asked Antonia.

'I…I will be back,' said Aida, and rushed off at once, off the terrace, along the alley, past the orchard, towards the mountain. She heard the old woman shouting and hid in the bushes to hear what she was saying.

'Aida, stay here, there are mines there! You don't know the area! Pedro will be coming in five days. Aida, use your head, at least wait for Josip! Aida?'

But Aida had no intention of going down again. She put a hand to her heart to calm it down. It was dreadful to hear Antonia begging, dreadful to imagine her in the loneliness of her house. Aida thought of her own mother. She had run away from her in almost the same way.

She would never forget the pale face behind the window of the bus. The bus had been full of Muslims, who had been driven out of Tuz and were on their way to Croatia with nothing but hand-baggage. On the way the convoy had been stopped at a control point on a mountain pass. Two girls, one of them Aida, had been ordered to get out. From nervousness they had laughed foolishly as they waved to their anxious families on the bus. 'Back in a minute, Mum.' Aida had formed the words soundlessly with her lips. But when she was standing in the guardhouse, to her horror, she heard the coach driving away. The other girl had begun to cry. 'Quiet, Turks!' someone shouted. They were tied up and put in a jeep, which followed the bus for a short distance, then turned down a bumpy side street. A boy of about eighteen or at most nineteen was at the wheel. Aida was so frightened that she had not recognized him.

He stopped, grabbed her arm and drew her away from the jeep. 'Aida, get away!' he hissed. 'But don't tell anyone what happened.'

Hearing her name, she looked him in the face and suddenly recognized him: Radomir, a boy from her school in Tuz. 'Go now!' he told her, after untying her wrists, but she had been too confused to understand. What was she doing on a mountainside, with a harsh wind blowing? She wanted to return to the bus. 'No good!' he told her. 'I was supposed to take one girl from the bus, as a sweetheart for my Commandant. He's bored, you know. I took two. Go now. You can still make it. Go!'

'What about the bus?' she stammered.

'The buses are going to the camp in Banjsko, men and women separately. Aida, get away, now!' And he suddenly turned and ran back to the jeep. Aida sat down, in spite of the bitter wind and dreary surroundings. And then, bit by bit, she began to see the truth. Her mother was going to a prison camp, the other girl would be abused, and she had been saved by a schoolfellow, who had his eye on her. 'Forgive me!' he shouted before he drove away.

She could not do that, not ever. But she could not forgive herself either. From the place where she had been taken off the bus by a trick, it was no more than ten kilometres to Banjsko prison camp, but she had been so frightened of the Chetniks that instead of running back to her mother, she had run further away from her.

As now, from Antonia. She narrowed her eyes and thought she could see the woman and the dog running through the village, stumbling over the rubble. She turned away guiltily. How could Antonia ever understand her deathly fear when the men were there? Singing, drinking and telling jokes, while she lay on her stomach behind her bed. For hours. She knew what Chetnik men did with Muslim girls. If just one of those drunks had come into the hall and looked behind the partition, they would have found her. And they would be coming back, now or in a day or two, to drink Jovo's slivovitz. Aida wiped the sweat from her forehead and took a couple of deep breaths. The stabbing pain in her breast gave way to a feeling of liberation. She had done the right thing. Brodište really was a trap. She must break away, in order to free herself. A pity she had left her jacket hanging in the kitchen. She would need it.

The dog was the first to hear the whistle. High, low, high, low. Twice. He raised his head joyfully to greet Josip. Josip meant water! 'Quiet!' said Antonia. 'Hush!' But she had to lean back and hang on to control the dog.

That was how Haris and Josip saw her, tottering through the village. They put down the jerry cans and looked at each other in surprise. 'Can I help?' asked Josip. He took the dog from her, while Haris lugged the jerry cans along on his own the rest of the way. They noticed the paper at once, lying on the garden table.

63

'A new one,' said Haris, 'from last week!'

'What's that doing there?' asked Josip.

Antonia sighed. 'Please give the dog some water first.'

'Where is the girl?' asked Haris.

Josip looked at the paper, and from the paper to the dog, whose tongue, as big as a shoe-horn, was hanging out of his mouth. In the distance they heard the last growl of the artillery.

'Actually we came...' Josip began, but thought better of it and said something else, 'We have come to fetch you, Aunt. Mila is already making a bed for you. It's getting too dangerous down here. Please come with us!'

'Now?'

'Yes, now!'

'What about the water?'

Josip looked silently at Haris, reproach in his eyes. They had brought the water in case she decided to stay – but she must not stay. It would not do!

'For goodness sake give the dog a drink,' said Aunt Antonia wearily. 'I can't come up, Josip. Aida has run away, just now, and yesterday Pedro came. My house is stuffed with supplies. And he's coming back in five days' time to pick up the girl and give her a lift to the coast. And this is the moment she chooses to run away!'

Josip and Haris sat down, nonplussed. Especially Josip, who had already decided how he was going to pilot his aunt over the steepest parts of the path, was quite dazed and said nothing more. Antonia rolled herself a cigarette. Napoleon lapped up the water, and Haris gnawed his lips. They sat on the terrace like a big still life, while it grew later and later, and also more and more dangerous.

'Listen, I've got an idea,' said Haris. 'I'll go and look

for the girl. She knows me, she's seen me. And you, Josip, you bundle up rice, beans, oil and so on – and bandages for Ramiz.'

'And then?' asked Josip.

'I may not be able to persuade her to come back to Brodište, but that might not be very sensible anyway. Not even for a few days. This afternoon the devils reduced Izvor to ruins. The church, the wooden mosque, the houses. They'll have to celebrate that, of course, and they know there's drink here.'

'But what then?' asked Josip again. 'Assuming you find her, do you want to persuade her to come up the mountain with us? She didn't want to last time either.' This was not a straightforward question: it was not about the girl, but about the word 'either'. Josip could not bear the idea that Haris could persuade Aida, when he had failed with Antonia.

'I'll try,' said Haris. 'I'll look till it's dark. After that I'll wait to help you carry the rice and tins up the mountain.'

'Be careful, boys,' said Antonia anxiously.

'More important for you to be careful!' Haris drank some water and stood up. His determined expression had vanished. 'Antonia,' he said, 'I think Josip is right. You must get away from here. I…'

'That's enough, lad, now go! I'll fill them up again, and then decide what to do.' Antonia smiled at him and for a moment her perfect teeth flashed very charmingly in her old face.

# Chapter 8

Haris thought the girl was cool. He had seen her only briefly, but had observed her attentively. He was thinking of her and of the mines when he climbed the Gora. Most of the mines had been buried in the maize fields and orchards to prevent the farmers from harvesting food. But mines had also been laid in the meadows and woods, which was why the boys always stuck to a fixed route which they had marked out the first time with scraps of cloth, but now knew by heart. Haris had left this route because he suspected that Aida was hiding at the edge of the wood. He stared tensely at the ground, placing one foot before the other like an old man. Now and then he stopped and called softly, 'Aida, where are you? Aida, it's me, Haris.' But there was no answer.

He noticed anxiously that the sun was going down, or rather, that Brodište was 'going down'. The days lasted much longer at the top of the mountain. There he stood, in a meadow full of fragrant, flowering shrubs, with bees skimming over them. The land belonged to them and the butterflies, the people had tossed it away. 'Aida!' he called dejectedly. He turned away; he must go back.

Step by step, as he had come, he walked down again, and he was on safe ground when he tried once more: 'Aida, where are you?'

'Here.'

He stopped abruptly. 'Where?'

'Here,' the girl repeated, standing up from the blackberry bushes where she had been hiding. She sucked blood from a scratch on her hand to avoid meeting his eye.

'Have you been here all the time?'

'Yes. I didn't know you were looking for me.'

Haris shook his head. 'Well, really!' This was crazy; he would so much have liked to say something nice but the tension he had been feeling for the last hour was suddenly released now that he had found her down here with just a couple of scratches. 'So I walked through a mine field for nothing?'

'I didn't know you were looking for me,' Aida repeated, 'or perhaps I would have said something.'

Haris calmed down. 'I thought you were at the edge of the wood, that's why I was worried.' At last she looked at him. At first he thought she was blushing, but then he saw that the sun had reddened her cheeks. 'I hear you may be getting a lift?'

She nodded.

'So why did you run away?'

'I didn't run away. I'm waiting here until the Blues drive to the coast again. I don't want to go back to that room.' She suppressed a shudder. All her body heat had risen to her fevered face.

'Take your jacket,' said Haris, seeing that she was cold. He quickly unknotted the jacket tied round his hips and walked over to the bushes to put it round her shoulders. But she stepped back.

'I'm not doing anything,' he said. 'I'm just giving you your jacket. I had gone as far as the orchard when Antonia called me back and told me to take the jacket.'

'Was she angry?' asked Aida.

'No. Shaken, sad, a bit worried, not only about you, but also about the Spaniard who promised to take you along. And she has all that food in the house.'

'What has food got to do with it?'

Haris laughed, which completely changed his frowning boyish face.

'Ah,' he said softly, 'it's not really funny. Josip wants his aunt to come and live on the Gora. That's really what he's wanted for weeks, and she's been resisting all that time. But after the shooting this afternoon he simply went to fetch her. I had to go with him because of the animals and to help carry bedding. The goat, the dog, his aunt, you, we were going to take everyone up there.'

'Me too?' stammered Aida.

'If you wanted to, but you weren't there, and Antonia doesn't want to leave her house while it's full of food.'

Aida zipped up her jacket and freed herself laboriously from the thorny bushes. She ignored Haris's outstretched hand.

'And now?'

'That's what Josip asked: when you've found her, what then? You can come up the mountain with us. We have a telescope to keep an eye on the country round Brodište. As soon as the Blue Helmets come back we'll bring you down again. There is a look-out on the peak from which you can see the village and...'

'And Antonia?' she interrupted him.

'She's staying until you get a lift.'

Aida was sitting down now, dazed by all these ideas. How could she go up the mountain, when the woman was staying in the village for her sake?

'And,' Haris continued, 'until Josip and I have moved all the supplies from the house. Then we hope she'll see sense. Josip sometimes gets in such a state about his aunt

69

that he can't sleep. He's worried about Antonia. She is his mother's sister.'

Mother, thought Aida. Wasn't it bad enough to have left one mother in the lurch? Surely she could survive a few last days in the village? She sighed, because if she was honest with herself she knew that she never wanted to enter Antonia's kitchen again, just as she never wanted to walk across a field or up the path here again. She had got herself in a fix, and the only way to keep faith with Antonia was to hide here – close to her – for the last few days. But who did that help?

From the corner of her eye she inspected the boy with the wild shock of hair who could laugh so infectiously and had striking eyes. Green eyes, she had noticed.

'All right, I'll come.'

Haris wanted to slap her on the back, but thought better of it. 'Great,' was all he said.

The shadows were lengthening round them and a light went on in the village. Feeble as it was, it attracted their attention at once. Aida sighed again: should she not say goodbye to the woman and thank her for her help?

'Is Josip still down there?'

'Yes, I don't know what's happened to him. He was only going to fetch rice and tins.'

'Perhaps they're still talking,' said Aida. And perhaps she ought to talk to the woman too, instead of disappearing helter-skelter up the mountain. She stood up hesitantly.

'Where are you off to?' asked Haris. 'Not to Brodište, not now!'

They waited for a time while the twilight turned into a dark, moonless night. Then, putting his fingers to his lips, Haris whistled: high, low, high, low, but the signal was useless. The dog would not recognize it – or would he?

Napoleon had started barking for a completely different reason. A car had stopped at the edge of the village and five men got out. One of them had a torch with which he helped the others to find their way to the house.

Aida screamed and felt a hand over her mouth.

'Don't scream!' whispered Haris. 'Quiet, please be quiet! We must leave here at once. Promise you won't scream any more?'

She nodded painfully, and the hand gripping her chin relaxed.

'Come on,' said Haris softly, 'give me your hand, yes, that's right, and stay right behind me. And please don't scream. We are going a little way up.'

Like two giant spiders they crawled together up the mountain. It was absolutely silent, except for the sounds of their breathing and of dislodged pebbles. Even Napoleon was quiet, but that alarmed more than it calmed her.

'Let's wait here,' said Haris, signalling to her to sit down. He had released her hand.

'Are you waiting for Josip?' asked Aida.

'Yes, of course, who else? We had agreed to carry the supplies together.'

Aida strained her eyes but could no longer see the single lighted house in the village. 'Where do you think he is?'

'Josip? Behind the partition.'

The word 'partition' was explanation enough. They

71

felt that they were each thinking the same thoughts.

'He's a boy,' said Aida.

Haris turned fiercely. She could not see it, but she could hear the grating of the sand.

'Just wait till you've seen Ramiz,' said Haris. 'Then you'll know what they do to boys!'

Trembling, she put her head on her knees and clasped her arms over it. She was not angry with him for snapping. She understood his anxiety for Josip and in some way it did her good that he was now reproaching himself as well. He had left Josip behind, as she had left Antonia.

'Listen, Haris,' she said, testing his name on her tongue. It was the first time she had used it. 'If he's behind the partition, everything depends on Antonia, and she knows what to do.'

Haris laughed feelingly: he might have been listening to himself speaking to his friend. 'Antonia certainly does,' he said. 'If necessary, Antonia can coax the stars from the sky. She can act an illiterate just as easily as a well-read Marxist. Like my mother, she's an actress, but Josip, oh, you don't know Josip!'

'What about Josip?'

'Josip is a neurotic. That's his good side as well, of course. He's more transparent than a pane of glass: you can see straight through him and still not know what he's planning. Or not planning, but doing. In town I've seen him hanging, swearing, out of the tram while it was being shot up by snipers. And I – my hands sweating – would be trying to pull him back in. And when we lived in Brodište he would sometimes get like that. One evening we were lying behind the partition because his

72

aunt had visitors. The men sang dirty songs and Antonia laughed. False laughter, of course, but he didn't understand that. I had to floor him without a sound, or he would have gone storming into the kitchen.'

Aida said nothing. She thought of her own reaction when she had seen the jeep, and was ashamed of her scream. But was the boy sitting invisibly beside her really so ice-cold? He talked a little too much for her to believe that.

They sat side by side for hours on the slopes of the Gora, growing more and more tired, cold and hungry. Haris saw the girl roll herself into a ball, trying to get a little sleep. He was faced with a big problem. Either he should take her up the mountain and return at first dawn to look for Josip, or he should wait half-way up. The third solution, to leave her here and go down to the village himself, was too risky. Any sound could send her into a panic and then she might leave the path and step on a mine.

'Aida.' He touched her very lightly and she grunted in her sleep. His empty stomach seemed to be answering, as it growled back. Haris made up his mind: 'Aida, we're going up'. Drunk with sleep, she struggled to her feet. 'Give me your hand, it gets very steep, and stay right behind me.'

When they went over the peak to the southern slopes, the east was brightening. 'Don't be frightened, I'm going to imitate a bird,' said Haris, laughing. 'For Mila and Ramiz, all right?'

She nodded, but ducked in shock when he imitated the harsh shriek of a bird of prey. Twice, and then once more, after a pause. 'That's our alarm clock with repeater function.'

The words sounded comical and inappropriate in these surroundings, which she could see only vaguely. Suddenly the flame of a torch was dancing a hundred metres away.

'Don't be frightened,' he whispered.

Aware of her nervousness, she tried to relax, but the face behind the torch was ghostly pale, with large, prominent eyes.

'Haris?' asked a girl's voice.

Aida started back when the torch was held up to her face.

'So this is her? Where is Josip?'

'Aida, this is Mila,' said Haris. 'Her bark's worse than her bite.'

In an embarrassed silence the girls sized each other up. Mila was smaller than Aida, but also broader and stronger. When they shook hands the difference was more easily felt than seen.

'Where is Josip?' asked Mila again.

'Down below, behind the partition. He was still with Antonia when the men came. I'm going back to get him. When the air is clear, he'll bring food up. The Blues have been back.'

'The Blues? Oh, wonderful!' said Mila. 'But you're not going straight down again, Haris. You must have some sleep first. Anyway, I've got a surprise for you: three rabbits! How about that?'

Aida followed the conversation with astonishment, as the girl, who was about Haris's age, behaved like his mother.

'Where do you sleep, actually?' Aida at last trusted

herself to ask.

'We used to sleep in the chapel,' said Haris, pointing to the black outlines of a small building on the slope. 'But it got too draughty for us and now we're cave-dwellers. We have lined the walls with turves and the floor with wood.'

'Come and see for yourself,' said Mila, crawling ahead of Aida through a split in the rock wall, into a space as big as a large room. The torch flare was just strong enough to shed a sparse light on the curiously shaped walls and ceiling.

Suddenly Aida saw the boy. He was sitting on one of the beds and gave her a friendly nod.

'This is my Ramiz,' said Mila, putting her arm across his shoulders. He was a Romany, a gypsy, or 'black', as many Serbs said.

Aida had secretly been expecting to see a boy with a dreadful deformity. You wait until you see Ramiz, Haris had told her. She put out her hand with relief. 'Hallo!' And not until she felt his left hand in her right did she see the thick, grey bandage round the right hand.

'Now I understand why it took so long,' Mila chattered on. 'Ramiz and I sat on the north flank with the telescope for hours, but didn't see a car. We thought you had decided to spend the night at Antonia's. Of course, we couldn't understand that, after yesterday's shooting. But that's what we told ourselves. Rabbit?'

Aida did not answer, so Haris nudged her. 'Would you like something to eat?'

Still Aida did not speak. She was sitting, in great confusion, on the edge of one of the beds: mattresses with proper sheets, blankets and pillows. Mila gave her a plate with two rabbit haunches on it.

'Tastes good, you try it,' said Haris.

'You too?' asked Mila.

'No, Mila, I couldn't get anything down. My nerves are shattered, honestly. Is there any water?'

Mila filled two mugs, which he and Aida emptied at once. Then Aida very cautiously bit into a haunch.

'Tastes great,' she said spontaneously. The rabbit was quite delicious after months of sardines and soya.

Mila nodded her approval and Haris smiled briefly before sinking back into his own thoughts. He was exhausted, but unable to sleep.

# Chapter 9

Mila extinguished the torch by rolling it to and fro in the sand. She groped her way into the cave and lay down beside Ramiz. From his restless tossing and turning she knew that he could not sleep, but in fact they were all awake. She was aware of it, although she could see nothing. Ramiz's wound was hurting, Haris was fearful for Josip, and the new girl, with her pretty face and good manners, was naturally wondering how she came to be here.

The boys might have missed it, but Mila had seen her frown. Aida had been thinking what most people thought the first time they saw Mila: what was a Serbian girl doing with a gypsy boy? It made Mila furious. She switched on her pocket torch and pretended to be looking for something in her clothes on the 'wardrobe', a tripod made of alder twigs. 'Are you comfortable?' she asked Aida.

'Yes.'

'Wonderful.' Aggressively she pointed the torch at the girl. 'Where do you actually come from? Ramiz and I come from Gorsko, a little place in East Bosnia. Do you know Gorsko?'

'No.'

'My father had a restaurant there. Before the war business was good, but not any more.'

'Oh.'

'Switch off the torch, Mila,' said Haris. 'Those are our last batteries.'

As she slipped back into bed Mila switched off the torch. In earlier times the family had done well. Her father had spoiled her and given her her own way in everything, until she had become a cheeky and uncontrollable child. When her parents could not do anything with her, the standard threat would come: 'Just you wait,' her mother would say furiously, 'the Terrible Gypsy will come and take you away!' In Mila's imagination the Terrible Gypsy was a dirty, stinking fellow, dressed in rags and with hair growing out of his nose and ears. But even worse things could happen. When she had really gone too far her mother would say angrily, 'Ludmila, that's enough! I'll give you away to the gypsy women!' After that sentence Mila would rush up to the attic to hide in the darkest, dustiest corner until her mother had calmed down. And then there was the fear when a gypsy woman came begging at their door. The threat did not pass until the woman had been sent away without her.

Much later, as she grew older, Mila realized that the women who went from door to door were not looking for badly-behaved children, but for something to eat, and dinars, money. And the other spectre, the Terrible Gypsy, also faded.

Beside her in the darkness Ramiz turned over with a groan. Mila wished Josip would come, and bring some bandages and disinfectant with him. She switched on the torch again and directed it at her friend. His forehead was hot and wet with sweat. As she leaned over him she saw Aida watching. Ruthlessly she turned the torch on her again.

'Awful, isn't it, I'm going out with a black. Now at last you can see the Terrible Gypsy face to face!'

Aida cowered under the blanket and Mila switched off

the torch before Haris could say anything.

Mila lay awake for hours while the others fell asleep. The new girl's light, fast breathing, Haris's snores and Ramiz's irregular panting turned the cave into a pump working at three speeds.

Through the cleft in the rock she saw the sky grow light. She got up quietly and walked across the brushwood that they called their parquet floor to the other side of the cave. No one reacted. Silently she observed Aida, lying with arms and legs outstretched, like a doll. She grinned and left the cave quietly. It was cold, the sun would not touch this place until later in the morning. or was she cold from a shortage of food? Her arms clasped round her shivering shoulders, she stood there, undecided, part of her wanting to impress the girl with piles of skinned rabbits, chestnuts and wild fruit.

But in the end her care for Ramiz won. She climbed over the peak and waited at the beginning of the path on the northern slope. At least the sun was shining here, which warmed her a little.

After about two hours – but she could not have said exactly, she had lost all sense of time – she heard someone coming up. She jumped nervously. 'Josip?' Josip appeared, looking deathly tired and hauling two heavy packages behind him.

'Hallo, Mila.' She kissed him as a matter of course, that was the way she was, Mila, the whirlwind. He sat down out of breath.

'No sleep, right?' she asked. 'What's it like down there now?'

Josip's lips tightened. He was scarcely able to control

himself. 'Why won't she go away? Why does she go on living there?'

'Was it bad?' asked Mila.

'To begin with she had left the wretched Croat paper lying about.'

'What paper? What do you mean?'

'She had got supplies,' said Josip, pointing to the packages, 'and with the food she also got one or two newspapers. Nationalist rubbish. Oh, what do the Spaniards know! They see the Pope on the front page and think everything is all right.'

'I still don't understand,' Mila interrupted.

'What is there not to understand? It's as clear as crystal! She hangs the icon on the wall and puts the Serbian bible on one corner of the unit. But there was the Croatian paper lying on the kitchen table, with reports of tourists in Istria, which Croats enjoy and Serbs loathe! A whole page full of views of people lying comfortably in the sun getting brown and making casual comments about the war through their beer. That was the first thing they saw.'

'Who?'

'The Chetniks, down there. Who else? Then they threw down the paper and saw the photograph of the Pope. Oh yes, and then of course some household effects had to be smashed up.'

Josip had seen nothing, but had heard it all from the dark cubbyhole behind the partition, which had made everything still worse. One of the men had read contemptuously from the paper. 'Lousy Pope!' the others had cried, smashing a pile of plates on the floor. In the noise no one had heard Josip leave the space behind the partition. Suddenly he was standing in the hall, peering fearfully into the kitchen. His aunt was standing in a daze among the broken crockery, but nothing had happened to her. Quite by chance their eyes had met, and he had seen her terror. 'Comrades, that is a mistake!' she had cried, taking the paper from the table and tearing it apart. The world news had fluttered like grey snow on to the shattered crockery.

'Can I help it if the Blue Helmets, who don't know a word of Croatian, bring this rubbish into my house? Come on, sit down, I'll get my dustpan and brush, and a bottle of Jovo's slivovitz and salami!'

Grumbling and only half convinced, the men had pulled out the chairs from under the kitchen table and as soon as they were seated Antonia had run out to the hall.

She grasped Josip by the hair, which was difficult, because she was so short, and hissed 'Idiot!' as she made an exaggerated clatter with her dustpan and brush. 'Get back to your corner, quick! And don't move, mind!' Then she hurried back to the kitchen to pour the drinks as quickly as possible. 'To Serbia!' They had clinked glasses.

'Was it stupid?' asked Josip, when he had finished. 'Would you have kept quiet if they had been swearing at your aunt and breaking her china?'

'No,' said Mila, 'probably not. But still, it was stupid. After all, you couldn't help your aunt. Did you spend the whole night crouched in the hall after that?'

'Yes, where else could I go? I didn't dare go back to the little room. I was afraid they might hear the partition moving, but also that someone might come out to the hall. I had an awful night. They didn't go until nearly morning. The kitchen was a pigsty. Plates, papers, all still lying around. I helped my aunt to sweep up the mess. She was ill. She had been smoking and drinking with them. Pah, it stank in there!'

'She really must leave there, Josip.'

'She realizes that at last, but she wants to wait for Pedro. He brought her to her senses with his plan of taking not only the girl but all of us along with him. The girl? Where is the girl?'

'Up there, and sleeping like a rose.' Mila felt the packages and lifted them to test their weight.

'Have you got dressings? Disinfectant?'

Josip nodded.

'What luck!'

Despite his protests she hoisted one package on to her shoulders before they went on. Josip imitated the bird of prey, but that was apparently not needed. He had scarcely closed his mouth when someone was rushing up the southern slope below him. It was Haris, his hair still tousled with sleep, furious with himself because he had not stayed up. He clambered up the slope on all fours and embraced his friend.

## Chapter 10

It was never light inside the cave house, the entrance was too narrow. All the same, they seldom used the pocket torch or the home-made oil lamp. Batteries and oil were expensive and they preferred to stay out of doors as much as possible.

'We did make a little fire to keep it bright and warm,' Mila explained, laughing. 'But then our parquet caught fire and we were almost roasted.'

Aida heard the chatter without really listening. Her eyes were following the circles Mila's hands made in the air as she removed Ramiz's bandage. She didn't want to look, but couldn't help herself. What was under the grey gauze dressing?

Josip had brought up the supplies and was now asleep in the cave, Haris was making breakfast. Everyone had a job to do and Aida felt superfluous and was in a bad mood. If she were to run away now, Mila might think that she was indifferent to her and Ramiz. If she stayed she would have to see it all – but wasn't that what she really wanted? The last turn of the bandage slid from the boy's hand and Aida turned pale and swallowed. Ramiz really did have three fingers! Where his little finger and ring finger had once been she saw stitched, but angrily inflamed wounds.

'Oh,' said Mila, concerned. 'Just what I thought. Wait a moment.'

She got up to fetch gauze and disinfectant. Ramiz looked from his hand to Aida, and gave a relaxed smile.

Shocked, she returned his look. Although he said nothing and she asked nothing, it was obvious to her that the loss of his fingers was terrible for him, much worse than the pain he suffered when Mila cleaned the wound. Mila said nothing, either, about what had happened to Ramiz. She dressed his hand again, the constant evidence of an event in the past.

Haris called out. He had cooked porridge in the kitchen behind the rocks. 'Coming?'

The kitchen lay in a shady hollow in the rock wall and consisted of iron bars laid over a stone fireplace, a box of cutlery and crockery and a jerry can with a tap.

'Porridge without lumps, Mila,' said Haris brightly. 'Shall we call Josha?'

'Let him rest. He didn't sleep all night.'

Hungrily they spooned up the porridge, keeping back a large portion for Josip.

'Where do you wash up?' asked Aida.

Haris had jumped to his feet. 'In the stream, but we'll go there later. First I'm going to show you something else. Only if you want to, of course.'

'What?' Aida saw Mila and Ramiz shaking their heads and laughing.

'Stones, *stećci*,' said Haris.

'Bogomil stones?' asked Aida.

He beamed at her. 'Do you know something about them? Have you read about them?'

'We talked about them at school.'

'A good school at last! Come on, you won't believe what you're going to see.'

Together they climbed down the Gora in a south-easterly direction. On that slope, which was almost completely bathed in sunshine, they sank up to their

84

knees in undergrowth. 'Aren't there any mines here?' asked Aida.

'Not up here! Further down, yes, where there are tobacco plantations. What do you know about the Bogomils?'

Aida was embarrassed. Was he questioning her? 'Weren't they foreign heretics?'

'What is a heretic?' asked Haris.

'How should I know? I'm an atheist.'

'Heretic comes from the Greek word which means a choice, or a school of thought. The Bogomils had a faith which diverged very strongly from the doctrine of Byzantium and Rome. They were against large-scale land ownership and the worship of saints. That is why they were persecuted.'

'Tough,' said Aida sarcastically.

'Yes, it was very tough for them,' said Haris, misunderstanding. 'In the eleventh century they put out the eyes of about fourteen thousand people in Macedonia. The emperor, who gave the order, was making fun of the Bogomil belief that they were enlightened by the Holy Ghost. If that was true, said the emperor, they didn't need any eyes. In the place where it happened there is now a lake, which is filled with their tears. At least, that's what the legend says.' He had been walking more and more slowly until now he was leaning against a tree to tell the end of his story.

But Aida's attention had wandered. When he had spoken about the eyes that had been put out, she saw Ramiz's hand again. Who had crippled him like that?

'Do you understand what that means to Bosnia?'

She gave him a guilty look. 'I wasn't listening just at

85

that moment.' She spoke rather timidly, but was suddenly gripped by a rage that surprised her. 'What do I care about the Middle Ages? I don't even understand this century! Fourteen thousand blinded Bogomils is bad, but they are dead and buried. Look what they did to Ramiz! That's today, it hurts today!' She thought he would be angry, but his light green eyes shone gently.

'Aida,' he offered, 'it's always easier to understand if you know the history.'

'Oh yes, I've heard that often enough – but what history? The history of the Serbs who were beaten by the Turks five hundred years ago, and that's why they're killing Muslims today? Or the history of the Bosnians who became Muslims under five hundred years of Turkish rule? Or the history of the Croats and their Austrian friends, who also had trouble with the Turks? History is nonsense, just like religion. It's always about the wrong things!'

Haris felt an inner excitement that he knew only too well. Smiling broadly, he looked at the girl and put out his hand hesitantly. Her red cheeks were glowing. For a second or two she let it be, then pushed him away. 'My face is bright red, yes or no?'

'More yes than no,' he admitted.

'Do you still want to go to the *stećci*?'

'Only if you do,' he replied.

They got up to walk the last part of the way to the graveyard. Haris had taken her hand and she didn't pull it away. He was so happy about that that he decided not to say any more about the Bogomils. It was difficult, because he was so full of it, but he controlled himself. The delicate, slender girl's hand in his gave him the strength to hold his tongue at last about things with which he had already bored the others silly.

'What a lot!' said Aida, when they reached the field with the stones in it.

'Yes, aren't there?'

She gave him a searching look and smiled imperceptibly. 'How do you know so much about it? Why does it interest you so much?'

'Perhaps you know my father? Edin Musanović? Before the war he was often on television. He is an art historian and an expert on *stećci*. He has written books about them.' From the way she was looking at him he knew what she was thinking. 'My father is bald,' he reminded her.

'But you have the same nose!' She began to laugh aloud when he held his nose.

He sat down on one of the stones, puzzled and then annoyed. He would never understand girls. When Mila came here she was obviously impressed and upset. She said little and never stayed long. But this girl had burst out laughing on the edge of the graveyard.

Aida noticed his mood changing, but could not stop laughing. It was nothing to do with noses. She was laughing because, after all those frightening events, her body simply felt the need to laugh. She stopped at last, feeling marvellously exhausted and relieved.

Haris did not speak for some time. He looked silently at the stones. 'It's still a cemetery.'

'Yes, of course. I'm sorry, but it wasn't that I was laughing about. But I don't have to be gloomy all of a sudden because I'm looking at *stećci*, do I?'

Haris turned, his face brightening as if by magic.

'That's true. The images on the *stećci* are nearly always cheerful. Do you know what I'd like? I'd like to take you home, to my father's study. It's a big room with a carved ceiling, huge bookcases and two worn old armchairs. We always used to sit there, talking. "Papa," I would say. "This is Aida! A stiff-necked atheist, but very sweet!"'

Aida blushed. 'Where are your father and mother?'

'At home, still in the same house. It gets shot at from the mountains by the papaks, and there's a half-baked sniper on the roof opposite. So all the windows are covered with black paper. Even if you pick at a tiny corner to look at the sky, you're in danger of the sniper taking aim and blowing a hole in your forehead.'

'And Josip, where did Josip live?'

'Next to us, in the same building. His mother is in a psychiatric clinic, but never let him know that you know that. And his father does his best to move to and fro between their house in the centre and the clinic without getting shot up.'

Aida silently pulled up blades of grass and wound them round her index finger. 'Doesn't Josip feel that he's left his father in the lurch?'

'No, you don't make a trouble any less by doubling it. His father positively begged us to leave Sarajevo. He was afraid Josip would do something stupid that might cost him his life. I told you about the streetcar from which Josip used to dangle in order to swear at the snipers. He often did that kind of thing. My father wanted us to leave, too, before we were old enough for conscription. My father is a pacifist, you know. He has his own ways of resisting. We thought it was awful to go away, but when your neighbours and your parents are always

88

asking you to go, you end up by going. A friend of my father's, a foreign diplomat, helped us to get out of town.

'Josip's father is alone now, of course, but he's supported by my parents and he doesn't have to worry about Josip. He doesn't know that Brodište is in ruins and that we're sitting on the Gora. Where do you come from, Aida?'

'From Tuz. Everyone had to get out.'

'Have you no family?'

'A brother, who lives abroad – luckily, I sometimes think. My mother is in Banjsko.' And the words tumbled out as, without taking breath, she told him of her flight and her guilt feelings after it.

'Good Lord!' said Haris. Taking her by the shoulders, he forced her to look at him. 'You mustn't think that, Aida! You must hope that the guy who took you off the bus has told your mother why he did it. But that's all. Imagine that you might have asked your mother on the mountain pass what she wanted you to do. You know the answer, don't you? You must always keep that in your mind!'

His hard, calloused fingers wiped away the tears that were now flowing freely. 'Filthy war,' he said, 'rotten, filthy war!'

He pulled her gently towards him and looked across the field of *stećci*, but his thoughts were somewhere quite different. 'Do you know what I'd like?'

Aida gave a big sniff. 'Yes, you'd like to take me to your father's study.'

'No, rather not,' he said laughing. 'In the evening, perhaps, after the meal, when he always goes and sits there. But first I would go to the Miljacka café and eat an ice on the boulevard. And then I would go to the park in Kovači, one of the older districts of the town. It's not there any more, the trees have been felled and vanished into multi-fuel stoves. Sarajevo is being burned up. All the cosy spots are disappearing. There's nowhere to go when you're in love.'

She released herself abruptly from his arm. 'Shall we have another look at the stones?'

He walked ahead of her through the lines of *stećci*. To begin with he had made sketches to mark the unusual finds, and by now he knew the whole field by heart. 'I come here every day, I try to brush and chip the accretions from the stones, that's why my hands are calloused. Why I do it I don't know. In town I often helped my father to clean *stećci* and we used to have good talks. Perhaps I do it because I miss him.'

Aida looked about her, amazed at the varied shapes of the stones.

'Notice the crosses,' said Haris. 'They are not harsh and stern, but round and mobile, like people. Here, look, circle-dances, a gravestone covered with dancing people!'

Aida nodded. When he told her what to look for, she could see it too. Some of the stones were very weathered and overgrown with moss. He walked on, like a museum guide with a tour to lead. But she stayed where she was. 'Haris?'

He turned round. 'Yes?'

'When were the stones made, and by whom? Why were the people living on a mountain?'

Haris walked back to the girl and laughed. He would tell her about it, but calmly, not all at once. She would

90

be surprised when she heard that she was as much a descendant of the heretics as he was.

# Chapter 11

Josip went down and back two or three times to bring up food from Antonia's house. The first time he was accompanied by Mila, the second time by her friend. But Josip did not feel so much at ease with the silent and introverted Ramiz. Ramiz had wanted to be a guitarist, Mila had once told him, and now, in the most literal sense of the word, that future had been cut off.

It had happened after Mila and Ramiz ran away from home. They had walked the first twenty kilometres, before being picked up by a refugee convoy. This seemed faster and safer, until a group of 'White Eagles' held up the bus. Shouting men in combat gear, with a white band round their heads, climbed into the crowded bus. 'We're going to do a show for you,' they announced, and then they had driven all the Muslim boys and the one 'Black' out of the bus and beaten them with rifle butts, sticks and bars. But a show has to have something edifying about it, so their leader gave a sermon. 'You Turks stick your bums in the air when you pray to Allah, but our God, the true God, doesn't care for that. Remember that! Real believers cross themselves, with three fingers, as we will show you.' And after that they had cut off the little finger and third finger of three of the boys.

Josip already knew the story, but when Mila went to Brodište with him he heard it all over again in detail. And when Ramiz came down next day, all the details re-echoed once again in their silence.

On that very quiet walk, Ramiz spoke at most four

times. There were days when he did talk, in short, staccato phrases; and there were days when he was silent, and then there were rows with Mila. Or more precisely, Mila had rows, because she was the only one making a fuss. She grumbled, complained and moaned and finally, in a last attempt to make her friend speak, she would begin to shout. But even Mila could not get through to him.

On the way to the village Josip was still trying to start a conversation, but on the way back he gave up. He was worrying about Antonia, waiting like a fat old maiden for her Spanish prince, while the fighting increased and one village after another was overwhelmed. The chance of Pedro coming back was shrinking as rapidly as her alcohol supply. But she refused to come up the mountain, although he had promised her that he would restore the old chapel. 'Nonsense!' she had exclaimed. 'You don't think the Blues are going to carry their food-aid up the mountain, do you? Either I stay down here in the village or we all go to Split. Autumn is coming, my boy, it will soon be winter! Do you know what the Gora's like in winter? You could build igloos up there. Chapels are the last thing you'll need.'

Of course she was right about that. As he climbed back up the mountain he could almost smell the coming autumn. August was like an over-ripe fruit, showing the first rot. He too would be glad to go to Split. It was not selfishness that made him beg her to move: he simply wanted to get her away from the soldiers and the explosions.

When he and Ramiz arrived at the top they found only

94

Mila waiting.

'Where is Haris? Where is Aida?' asked Josip, his eyes searching for the other two, who kept on leaving the group.

Mila had found a word for it: 'Oh, they're just Bogomilling,' she said with a wink.

It sounded like a card game or a sport, but it jarred badly. Josip was jealous. He had been the first to see Aida, but Haris, the Sun King, had monopolised her before he could exchange so much as a word with her.

The first time he returned exhausted from Brodište he had stolen off to the *stećci*. He felt thoroughly mean, spying on his best friend, but was he only good enough to act as a pack mule for the supplies, or as a confidant for Mila when Ramiz was not around? Then at the graveyard his self-pity was so great that he wanted to swear at Haris and punch him on the nose. He was really surprised to find them not paying attention to each other, but to the stones. Aida now had a small file as well.

That had been yesterday. Today Josip had no intention of returning to the graveyard. He would help Mila and Ramiz to unpack the supplies and hide them in the cave. They had been looking forward for weeks to the packets, bags and tins, but now that the food was there, the expected relief did not come. Their empty stomachs had diverted them from the chief problem: where were they to live when summer was over? The war in the valleys had sent them fleeing to the mountain, where the living was not too bad at all. That was why they had spent three months living like wild animals on the flank of the Gora. But the heavy, sweet scent of ripe fruit which Josip had first smelled in Brodište now lay on the mountain as well. It was the breath of autumn. They knew that they had to get away from here to the south-west, to the coast. Only Haris and Aida were not yet aware of it.

Within three days Aida's skin had turned from red to golden-brown, and her hair had bleached in the sun. And she had had a bath. On the evening of the first day Mila had taken her to the stream in the wood. 'It's cold,' she had warned, 'but it's necessary!' Then she had undressed and jumped into the water with a yell. Aida had looked round suspiciously. What if the boys were watching? 'If they're gawping, they'll get biffed on the nose,' said Mila, who could read thoughts. 'Take off your clothes and come in!'

The water was icy cold, made bearable only by hopping around, jumping and shrieking. Not for long. Mila soaped her back, she soaped Mila's. Quickly, quickly, as their fingers turned numb. When they had dressed again, blue and shivering on the bank, Mila said: 'Aida, I've got strips of sheet, if you…well, you know.'

'Menstruate?' asked Aida.

'Yes, you know what I mean,' said Mila, who combined a prudish vocabulary with a passionate desire for freedom.

Aida wondered curiously if Mila was actually sleeping with Ramiz, but the thought made her uncomfortable: how would it be possible, with five of them in that space? Last night she had been unable to sleep for hours as she listened tensely. But she had heard nothing. She might be readier than Mila to use words like 'menstruation' or 'intercourse', but they were and remained words from biology lessons. In practice, on the Gora, they took on a quite different meaning. She was the youngest of them all and felt like a cuckoo in the nest, with three fathers and one mother.

By day she helped Haris to clean up the *stećci*, though of course it was pointless. There was fighting in the valleys round about and no connoisseur or museum director would come up here to look at their work. But cleaning up the *stećci* filled their days and their conversations.

'Haris, you've told me so much about doves, suns and deer, but I'm interested in the people! Who made the *stećci*?'

'Just Bosnians like you and me. Perhaps you are actually cleaning a *stećak* belonging to your own family. The stones are five to six centuries old, but the gnostic sect of the Bogomils is older, and used to have a different name. It's based on the ideas of Paul, the apostle in the New Testament.'

Aida's face froze.

'Listen, this is interesting, even for atheists! Paul travelled a long time in Arabia, which is why you can find Arabian motifs on the *stećci*, such as crescent moons in the form of a grail. Bogomils didn't make pictures of saints, they expressed themselves in symbols. The heart of Paul's message was...'

'Please,' Aida interrupted, 'no sermons. Please!'

'The heart of Paul's message,' Haris repeated, 'was that people should not be guided by laws but by their own conscience. That's how he founded a movement which was always anti-authoritarian. Why should anyone with money and power, an emperor or a pope, have more rights than anyone else? Throughout history there have been people who proclaimed Paul's ideas. Like the Manichees, who penetrated as far as Egypt and even China.'

'Oh well, that didn't help much.'

'And how!' cried Haris. 'Because local rulers persecuted and murdered them. After all, power is powerful.'

'But God is all-powerful, isn't he? Couldn't he have helped the Bogomils and us a little bit more? How can I believe in a god who lets my mother be put in prison? She has never done anyone any harm, but she's in a concentration camp two hours from here! The god who allows that is a devil!'

Haris was startled by her fierceness. She had flung the little file away and was pointedly sitting with her back to him.

'Aida, something else. Let me finish. Please!'

'You never stop talking!'

He sat down helplessly beside her. 'What you're thinking isn't new. Millions of people before you have wondered why God, if he is good, allows all this misery. There are three possible answers: God is not all-powerful, not good, or he doesn't exist. You believe the last. But then how are you to explain things like solidarity and mercy? They're not genetic developments in humans or something?'

'What do you believe, Haris?'

'Me? I don't know. Do you know what the Bogomils thought? They believed that God had two sons, one bad and one good, called Satan and Christ. The bad one created the world and after that the second son tried to help human beings.'

Aida laughed grimly. 'So Tuz, Brodište and the capital are destroyed by family quarrels? And God can't do a single thing about his first son?'

'God can't punish, the Bogomils say, only provide good examples.'

'God can't punish, but he lets my mother be punished, and Ramiz and Mila and Josip. Very consistent, don't you think? Why can't God punish?'

'Because,' said Haris, 'because...' He got no further. He was not prepared for her sharp questions. 'Punishment is negative, the Bogomils say. A god is good and only does good things.'

'Just like the United Nations,' said Aida. 'They don't do anything about peace enforcement either, just hand out food.'

Haris shrugged his shoulders. 'I give up. You win,' he said.

'No, I lose! I've lost everything I loved. Where did these crazy Bogomils come from? Why did they have those ideas?'

'In the Middle Ages Bulgaria was the heresy centre of the world. Manichees, disciples of Paul, they were all there. People who openly professed their beliefs called themselves Bogomils – Bulgarian for beloved by God. When they became too numerous the Emperor of Byzantium had them killed, and then the heresy spilled over here.' Haris spoke unwillingly. He had had enough of *stećci* and fancied some juicy rabbit.

But Aida tugged at the corner of his shirt and made him sit down again. 'And then we became Bogomils – the people of Bosnia, I mean?'

'The people, the nobility, the king, became Bogomils, yes. And they were persecuted too – by popes, patriarchs and emperors. Then the Turks came and all the heretics fled to the mountains, but after a few years they crawled out of their caves and were converted to Islam, the only church that had not persecuted them.'

'Interesting,' said Aida.

'Yes,' Haris agreed.


They walked back in silence to the cave, but only Ramiz was there. His face was sunburnt, like theirs, but three or four shades darker. 'Where are Josip and Mila?' asked Aida.

'Gone to Brodište, for the last time, they said.'

'In the evening?' asked Haris.

'They left half an hour ago.'

'But why?' cried Haris. 'We've got enough to eat here already.'

'Josip wanted to bring his aunt out – or try to, at least.'

'Is that why they both went?' asked Aida.

'You weren't there.'

'But we've got enough to eat!' shouted Haris. 'You should have stopped them.'

'I tried. Useless.'

Haris walked up and down nervously, tortured by guilt feelings, which he unleashed on Ramiz. 'It's so stupid to go down in the evening. You could have told them that!'

'Calm down!' Aida interrupted. 'Look where the sun is, they can get back before dark. If you make a fire, I'll cook for five.'

'Those donkeys,' grumbled Haris, but he put an arm

100

round Ramiz's shoulders. 'I'm sorry I shouted at you.'

'It's all right. Forget it.'

'How's your hand doing?'

Ramiz made a dismissive gesture.

'You've got Mila,' said Haris, 'that's not nothing.' He sketched the outlines of a girl with both hands, and immediately saw the unfortunate resemblance. But it was too late.

'Mila is Mila,' said Ramiz. 'A guitar is a guitar.'

They were eating supper when Mila appeared, tugging a rebelliously bleating goat on a rope. It was not yet dark, but the sun was already rolling away from the mountain, radiating a soft, violet light from the depths. Mila appeared on the mountain, dark against the setting sun. She tugged savagely on the rope, but Svetlana was thirsty and tired, and braced herself with all four legs.

Haris sprang up with a cry, the plate slipping from his lap. 'Wow, he made it! Josip did it!' He rushed towards Mila. 'Are they coming? Can I help? Shall I go to meet them?' But he stiffened when he saw her tired, drawn face.

'Take this beastly goat, will you? I've got blisters on both hands.'

He took the rope at once. 'Has something happened? Aren't they coming? For goodness sake tell me!'

'First I must have something to drink,' she said. 'And that beast must have something, too.'

Instead of pulling the unwilling goat along, Haris put his arms round her stomach and carried the struggling animal to the cave as fast as possible. 'Water!' he commanded Ramiz and Aida.

Sensing that something bad had happened, they obeyed nervously. When the goat had drunk and been tied to a tree and Mila had also emptied two mugs, there was a tense silence. The other three gazed at Mila.

'Antonia is ill,' she said suddenly. 'Very ill, she can barely speak. She's in dreadful pain, in her heart and her chest. She was lying on her bed when we arrived. Josip is staying with her.'

They looked at each other in dismay. 'But Mila,' said Haris, 'we were down there yesterday, and again this afternoon. Was she already ill then?' He heard himself saying 'we' as if he had been there.

'No, she was just as usual. This afternoon Josip even had another argument with her, about moving.'

'So why did he go down again?' asked Haris, making it sound as if Josip's return had made Antonia ill. His thoughts were twisting and turning, trying to avoid facing what he already knew. He, Musanović junior, had been busy fooling around with the *stećci* and a girl, while his friend toiled away and worried about Antonia.

'A premonition,' said Mila. 'He had a premonition. Late this afternoon he suddenly wanted to go down again, but of course with Aida or me as well. He thought Antonia would be more likely to listen to us than to him.'

'And then?' asked Aida.

'Then of course I went with him. Down in Brodište Josip whistled, for Napoleon, you know. But Napoleon didn't answer. We went ahead cautiously, not trusting the silence. The kitchen door of the house was shut, but when Josip whistled again we heard the dog whining inside. We thought: she's gone to the vegetable patch or the orchard or the goat. We were really very relieved until we went in.

'Napoleon behaved so strangely, whining and circling round us. And then we heard groans. She was lying, fully dressed, on the bed, her arms crossed on her chest as if she had to hang on to something. Her fists were clenched and she was groaning all the time. It was dreadful!'

'And then?' whispered Aida. 'Could you talk to her?'

'Not right away,' said Mila. 'Josip was completely

confused. He seemed to be groaning with her. He sat on the edge of the bed and tried to hold her hands, but she was all tensed up. I didn't know what to do at first either. I gave Napoleon some water and soaked a cloth for her, and hunted through all the cupboards and drawers for aspirin. I found two headache pills and tried to give her them dissolved in water. Half of it trickled down her chin. She was in such pain, such frightful pain!'

'But where? Could she tell you?' asked Aida.

'In her chest and arms, but especially in her chest. She was glad we had come. She didn't say so, but I could see it in her face. When it grew dark Josip said I must go back to the mountain, and Antonia called: "The goat, the goat!" At first we didn't understand her. I asked if I should take the goat with me, and she said: "Yes, please." I thought it was scary. I was afraid of going the wrong way, and the creature didn't want to come. And all the time I had to keep looking round at the house, and then I would see her before my eyes again.'

It was dark when Mila finished her story. They sat in a circle, like four black silhouettes. Aida overcame her shyness and crawled over to Mila, cautiously laying a hand on her arm. 'Hey, it's all right now, isn't it? You got up here safely.'

The two boys stirred at last. Ramiz took Mila in his arms and rocked her like a child, murmuring endearments. Haris called out that he was going to get the torch. 'Why?' asked Aida, in alarm.

'I'm going down, that's why! Don't wait for me. I shan't be back until morning at the earliest, or towards noon.'

'What are you going to do there?' asked Aida, watching as he checked all the supplies in the cave with his torch. 'Mila!' he called impatiently. 'Mila, didn't we get any aspirin from the Blues either?'

'No,' said Mila, 'only dressings and disinfectants. Nothing for pain. Not even for Ramiz.'

Swearing under his breath, Haris put on a pullover. 'So don't wait for me!' he said, pointing the lamp at their pale, grave faces and then at himself, with an artificial laugh. 'Everything's all right, you see? Calm as a cod on a slab. See you tomorrow!'

Aida's eyes followed his dark shadow moving up the slope, standing out for a moment on the peak before disappearing from view on the other side. With a sudden surge of feeling she ran after him.

'Haris?' she shouted down the northern slope and saw the torch light up about fifteen metres below her.

'What is it?'

She was breathing fast and irregularly. She wanted to say that she had been much too aggressive that afternoon. 'You will be careful?' she begged.

He sighed. He thought he was a fool and didn't need any comments to confirm it. 'What else!' he replied grumpily. 'Go and get some sleep, eh? I'll be really careful, sure!' He came back, gave her a quick kiss on the cheek and vanished down the slope. She stayed there, watching, for a long time. Now and then she saw the flash of the torch. 'Oh God, let it be all right!' she muttered. 'If you can only do good things, please send an ambulance, a doctor, painkillers, help!'

As time went by the pain seemed to lessen, but perhaps

Antonia was just so tired that she had no strength left for groaning. Josip had gone to the kitchen, lamp in hand, to open a tin. He ate the beans cold. To make up the fire or put on a saucepan was too much for him. As soon as he felt that he had to some extent filled his grumbling, empty stomach, he returned to the room, where a different emptiness threatened. It was the only room in the house that was still habitable. The walls were still vertical as they had been before the war, there were pictures there, of his Uncle Jovo and his aunt on holiday by the sea, and there were plenty of small ornaments. He set the lamp on the table by the bed and pulled up a chair. Antonia was still breathing loudly and irregularly, but she was less tense. Her hands were no longer clenched, but still lay on her chest.

'Would you like something to drink?' asked Josip. 'Can I get you another blanket?'

'No,' she panted.

The sound of her voice shocked him. Words came from her mouth in short jerks and gasps: 'Josha…go away from…Brodište…with the dog…the sooner…the better.'

'Don't talk too much. You've got to rest. Are there any pills left?'

'Won't help…any more… My heart…dear boy… Leave Brodište… All…'

'Don't talk rubbish! You'll get well again. You're incredibly strong. You need rest.'

'I shall…rest… Don't…be sad.'

'But you are terribly strong! This afternoon there was nothing wrong with you. You waved when I went up the Gora. Everything was as usual.'

'I was tired … I lay down…just for a short time… The pain woke me…'

Josip desperately pulled out the drawers of a bedside table, looking everywhere, in all the places where Mila had already searched.

'Aren't there any more pills anywhere?'

'Josip…my boy, sit down…'

He sat down, weeping, on the chair. 'You're fantastically strong.'

'Not now…my boy… Don't be sad…' She smiled through her pain. 'I'll be moving…after all…perhaps…'

Josip slipped from his chair to hug her to him, his tears running down her cheeks, until her body lost its tensions and relaxed. Suddenly she was lying quite peacefully.

With a corner of the sheet he wiped her wet cheeks. He combed her grey hair, straightened her crumpled dress, and when he felt that her fingers could be straightened he took her hands from her heart and folded them loosely lower down. Then he left the room. Napoleon whined and barked. Josip talked to him quietly, put on his lead, blew out the lamp and went outside. But the dog lifted his head and howled heartrendingly.

If the trash were to come to the village now, he would be for it – but suddenly this was of no importance. With the dog, which from time to time lay down without warning so that Josip stumbled over him, he walked towards the Gora. Napoleon's grief comforted him. The dog was making the fuss that he would have liked to make.

They climbed the mountain by stages. Josip had to sit down again and again to calm the dog. He tickled him under the chin, stroked his head and back and patted his sides, until he began to calm down, and only whined now and then. Both of them, the dog and Josip, jumped when a beam of light struck them out of the darkness.

'Josip, it's me, Haris!'

They ran to meet each other.

'And?' asked Haris anxiously.

'She's dead.' The words fell like lead into the night.

Haris did not know what to say. He put his arm round Josip's shoulders, stroked Napoleon and was silent. They sat side by side for several minutes while the fact sank in: Antonia was dead. There was no more Brodište.

'Come,' said Haris finally, 'you must get some sleep, or at least lie down. Come on.' He pulled his friend up by the arm and took the dog from him, just as he had taken the goat from Mila. Now and then he switched on the torch, but they climbed the greater part of the way in darkness.

Ramiz, Mila and Aida were waiting for them up above. They were standing at the end of the path, like the spectators at the finishing line. When they saw the two boys and the dog there was no need to ask questions. Like a funeral procession, they returned to the cave, in which a small lamp was burning. Mila made tea, Ramiz gave the dog some water and Aida spread rusks. Scarcely a word was spoken. They restricted themselves to: 'Tea?' 'Sugar?' 'Something to eat?' And as the spoons tinkled in their cups, they watched Josip's tear-streaked face and glassy eyes.

It was light when they went to sleep, aware that the dearest liaison officer with the world down below had died the night before. They could not leave her lying there. They would have to bury her somewhere.

# Chapter 13

Mila was milking the goat. Aida saw the milk squirting into a pot and shook her head admiringly. 'How do you know all these things? Did you live on a farm?'

'No, we had a café restaurant, "The Old Bridge", in the centre of Gorsko. When I was sixteen my father thought I had learned enough and took me out of school. I had to help my mother in the house. That's why I can skin rabbits, milk a goat and bake pastries. My father had a business where everything possible was done by hand. "Fresh" and "home-made" were his trade marks. The meat on the menu should really have been still bleating when a customer ordered it, and the lettuce should still have been in the ground. My mother was quite fed up with it, but I wasn't, it suited me. I had just begun to work when the war began and a lot of customers stayed away. People didn't have the money to eat out. They only came in to drink. There was nothing much to do in the kitchen. Svetlana is out of milk. Look at that, just a splash of milk at the bottom!'

Aida shrugged her shoulders. What did that matter? Goat's milk! But Mila chattered on, about udders and fat content. That was her way of calming her nerves. Perhaps the best way.

She and Ramiz were not talking, Josip was worn out and Haris was talking to himself. They were all trying in their own way to work through Antonia's death, which seemed quite unreal. It was tempting to believe that one of them had had a dream and told it so vividly that the others dreamed it as well. But they had only to look at the animals to know the truth. Both frightened and restless, the goat and the dog tugged awkwardly at their long ropes. No wonder the goat gave so little milk.

So they drank their coffee, black. After all, it was pure luxury to have coffee again. The rusks with fish paste were left untouched: no one was hungry.

'It's getting hot,' said Haris. 'We shouldn't wait too long.'

The others shivered. No, they should not wait too long. Who knew what would happen, if the men in the jeep got there ahead of them?

'Where shall we bury her?' asked Mila. 'In the orchard, perhaps?'

'Why down there?' asked Haris. 'I suggest we bring her up here. If we all help, it will work. We can make a stretcher with two thin tree trunks and a blanket.'

They looked at him, baffled. Only Josip seemed not to have heard.

'Up here?' stammered Aida.

'Why not?' Haris blushed. 'Down there everything is dirty and broken, but up here we can easily make her a proper grave. It would be safer for us, too.'

Mila sucked thoughtfully on her lower lip as she redid her dark, shoulder-length hair in a pony-tail. 'What do you think, Ramiz?'

'It's peaceful up here,' said Ramiz. 'Perhaps too peaceful, when we've gone. There will be snow, there will be ice. I don't know.'

Aida had an idea. 'Haris?' She waited until he looked at her, then asked without beating about the bush: 'Do you want to bury her with the *stećci*?'

'Oh no!' cried Mila, turning pale at the idea of burying Josip's aunt in a place which she regarded as haunted.

'What is it now? Why are you staring at me?' said Haris irritably. 'Is my suggestion so crazy? We mustn't pretend, we must see things as they are. In Brodište the most we can do is make a hollow to lay her in, and even that is awkward. Do you think it's very respectful to put Antonia in the ground like a dead animal?'

'Don't talk like that!' shouted Aida.

'It's hypocrisy not to call things by their names. If she's here we can make a coffin and she will be getting one of the most magnificent gravestones in the world, a stone worthy of Antonia. She was Catholic, Orthodox, Communist, perhaps Muslim as well. She was everything and nothing in particular. She was beloved of God.'

'No, Haris!' cried Aida. 'She was no Bogomil!'

'What are you talking about?' Mila interrupted.

'He's gone mad!' said Aida.

'Why mad?' asked Haris. Deeply hurt, he looked at the girl who had wormed his secret thoughts out of him and then declared him mad. 'What's mad about it? Explain!'

'Antonia was not a Bogomil. She may have had things in common with the people up here, but she was not a Bogomil and you mustn't turn her into one!'

'You are both mad!' Mila cut in. 'That's what you get from your *stećci*. Stop quarrelling. Let Josip decide. She was his aunt!'

She looked at the one person who had not spoken. He looked wretched and had not really been listening. Mila told him in a few words what they had been talking about. She said nothing about the *stećci*, but simply mentioned the possibilities: up here, or down in the village.

113

Without answering, Josip walked into the shadowy cave. They stared after him in surprise, but he came out again immediately with something in his hand. He was walking slowly and unsteadily, as if he had been drinking. 'Here,' he said, 'my uncle. I took the picture out of her bedroom last night. There were about ten photos of him there.'

They looked at the photograph, confused by the picture of the laughing Antonia beside a tall man with white, youthful-looking hair. 'That was taken on the island of Hvar, wasn't it?' asked Mila. 'We had our holidays there too.'

Aida and Haris were shocked by Mila's tactlessness.

But Josip just smiled. 'Yes,' he said sadly, 'Uncle Jovo and Antonia always went to Hvar. That's where they met.'

'Why are you showing us the photo, Josip?' asked Mila.

'Oh, I thought…we didn't talk about it yesterday, it simply wasn't possible then. But the best place to bury her is beside Uncle Jovo.' He lifted his swollen eyelids and looked at them in turn. 'Or do you think it's too dangerous?'

They set out in the early afternoon, when the worst of the heat was over, carrying two shovels. There was another behind the house. They would look for anything that would help them to dig. They had so little time. Luckily the cemetery lay a little higher than the village, so that in case of danger they could retreat to the Gora. Aida avoided looking at Haris on the way down. She was feeling anything but triumphant, because what he said was quite true: they could have buried Antonia far more safely up above, but it would have been a lonely grave in a wretched place. After all, Antonia herself had never been interested in the *stećci*. It would be dishonest both to her and to the heretics who had set up the stones to bury her in a Bogomil cemetery. He must understand that!

When the path narrowed and Haris was walking ahead of her she could observe him freely. He looked thinner and smaller than usual – or was that only because she was walking above him and she could see his black curls bouncing at ever step? He was a nice boy. He meant well, and he too had loved Antonia.

When they reached the bottom Josip put his fingers to his lips to whistle as usual and in their nervousness they couldn't help laughing.

'You stay here,' said Haris, 'and Josip and I will bring her out.'

'Is she in her bed?' asked Mila. 'I would like to see her there again. May I?'

They entered the house two by two while the others watched the road. First Josip and Haris, then Mila and Ramiz, then Aida and Haris again. They stood silently by the bed in which Antonia seemed to be sleeping. She looked remarkably peaceful. 'Are you cross with me?' asked Aida. Haris shook his head. 'No, I'm frightened. We've got to hurry!'

Ramiz took the shovels, the girls carried the bedding and Haris and Josip carried Antonia out of the house. In the graveyard crickets were chirping, as they had the first time Aida had been there. It was still suffocatingly hot down here. 'Here,' said Josip, panting. 'My uncle's buried here.' He nodded towards the cross. No more was said, but the boys pulled off their shirts and began to dig. The sand fell on the earth from their shovels with dull thuds, while Mila and Aida shakily wrapped the body in the bedclothes. After that they helped the boys, one with a snow shovel, the other with a dustpan. They worked hard, pausing only briefly to wipe the sweat from their foreheads. After two hours the grave was deep enough and they let Antonia slide slowly into it.

Josip took a handful of earth, then Haris, then Mila and the others. Each of them dropped their handful on the flowered linen. They had no more time to honour her. The sun was vanishing behind the Gora.

They had to fill in the grave at once and set up the cross, a simple wooden one, on which they had scratched: Antonia Rodić-Poljarević, 1940–1994, special feature: angel.

Mila laid apples, sweets and flowers on the grave. Ridiculous, but it touched them all.

'We must go,' said Haris, after a quick glance at the road.

But Josip wanted to get something else from the house. A couple of pictures, he said, mementoes.

Haris frowned as he watched him go. 'Once in there, he will probably turn everything upside down. He's quite mad enough! You go straight up the mountain – we'll catch you up.'

'Shall we wait?' asked Ramiz, when Haris had run across to the house.

'Yes, we'll wait,' said Mila.

Aida sniffed nervously. 'What's he looking for now?

Why is it taking so long?'

'Things from her room,' said Mila. 'Shells, little boxes, rings, and of course he can't make up his mind, or can't find what he's looking for.' Mila too was nervous.

As they waited they looked alternatively at the road and the house.

'There they are!' cried Ramiz, but he did not mean the two boys. The jeep came driving up the road!

Ramiz was soaked with sweat. 'I'll go and warn them,' he said. 'If I hurry, I'll just make it!'

'No, Ramiz, don't!' screamed Mila, but her friend had already raced into the village, zigzagging through the ruins to Antonia's house. At the same time the jeep was jolting its way further into Brodište.

'I'm not going to look,' said Mila. 'Tell me what's going on.'

'Ramiz is in the lane,' said Aida. 'Three or four men are getting out. Ramiz is on the terrace, he's inside. The men are coming into the lane!' She stopped, she could not go on. The blood was pounding in her temples and throat, and she had to blink to rid herself of the veil before her eyes. She saw the boys come out as the men walked onto the terrace, and turned away, moaning.

At the same moment she was grabbed by Mila. 'Sssh! Keep quiet!' With her strong hands she held Aida's mouth, keeping her in a stranglehold for minutes. 'It's over! They've got them! Do you get it, it's over!'

Aida goggled at her, while the back of her head was being pushed ruthlessly into the sand. Was this the same girl who just now had not dared to look?

'It's over,' said Mila again, her voice rougher than usual. 'It's no good screaming.' Slowly she relaxed her

117

hands, and when at last she let go the imprint of her fingers was left on Aida's cheek.

'Where are they?'

'Still in the house, all of them.'

'Seven of them in the kitchen?'

'Yes,' said Mila, 'or in Antonia's room. Or else the boys had just time to crawl behind the partition, but that would be a miracle.'

Aida sat up and shook the sand out of her hair, gazing fearfully down at the house. As long as the door was still shut she and Mila could believe in a miracle, but the door opened, and they saw the Chetniks coming out with the boys. All three had their hands tied behind their backs. The boys stumbled as they walked – they had probably been beaten. The men drove them on impatiently to the jeep, into which they could squeeze only with difficulty. When the jeep drove away their bare arms were hanging outside.

Mila stared furiously after them. 'The day will come,' she said, shaking with anger, 'when I'll make them pay for that! For all their filthy tricks. I shall never forgive them for what they did to Ramiz. And Antonia, and Haris, and Josip!'

Aida was silent, aware that Mila meant what she said.

They climbed up the mountain, because for the present there was nowhere for them to go except the Gora. Up at the top the sun was still shining as if in a different world. Napoleon barked and tugged at his lead and the goat went round in erratic circles. Mila gave them water and split wood for a fire.

'What are you doing?' asked Aida. 'You don't need to cook for me.' She sat in a daze in front of the cave, which

118

suddenly seemed much too big for them. She was reproaching herself: if she had backed Haris instead of arguing against him, how would things have gone then?

'I'm heating water. We must wash.'

Aida shrugged her shoulders. 'There's nothing we must do.'

'Really?' asked Mila, angrily. 'How do you think I'm feeling? Ramiz was my man, not a friend, much more. Through that business with his hand I lost half of him, and this afternoon, in that damned dump, the rest went too! As soon as he ran to the house I knew it was too late, he couldn't have made it, even by flying. I'm not crying, no, I'm not moaning, but that doesn't mean that here,' – she beat her chest – 'that I'm not hurting here!'

'We should have done what Haris suggested.'

'Antonia under a *stećak*? No!'

'Because of your childish belief in ghosts!'

Mila slapped Aida's face furiously. For a few seconds Aida held her hand to her burning cheek, then she jumped up and threw herself on Mila. They rolled across the ground, struggling, with the animals looking on. It was their terrible helplessness that was trying to vent itself in blows, swear words and tears. When the dog barked, they stopped. Aida felt her sore nose, Mila her scratched cheek. Exhausted and dishevelled, they lay side by side on their backs, staring at the sky.

'It's getting dark,' said Mila, snuffling. 'I'll heat some water.' And Aida went along to lend a hand.

## Chapter 14

They had several to choose from, but out of habit each lay down on her own mattress, and only then, with the other beds beside them but without Josip's snoring, Haris's dry cough and Ramiz's mutter, they realized that it was ridiculous to lie several metres apart.

'Are you asleep?' asked Mila.

'No, I don't think I can ever sleep again.'

'How's your nose getting on?'

'It's all right,' said Aida, half sitting up.

'Shall we push the beds together?'

Aida nodded, then added, 'Yes,' because it was dark in the cave. The night outside was actually less dark, as they could see from the lighter patch where the entrance was. 'Where did all this stuff up here come from?'

'Brought up from the houses in the village. A lot of it has burn marks, haven't you noticed?'

'No. Were you, Ramiz and you, up here a long time?'

'Seven weeks, I think. Before that a week in Brodište, when Antonia gave us a room with crooked walls. Did you sleep there too? You must have, there was nowhere else. But once the boozers had visited her I didn't trust myself to stay there any longer. I hate drunks! I've seen too many of them. My brothers always had to drag them out of the bar after holidays.'

'I thought you had a restaurant?'

'Until about eleven at night. After that only the bar was open. There were people there every day who wanted to listen to the music, because we had a house band, five gypsies, who played stunningly well. That brought in the customers. I always wanted to listen too, but my father was against it. I was only good enough for the kitchen. Until I was twelve I had a good time at home, but after that I had to help. After school, in the holidays and later on every day. The kitchen was behind the bar counter, but if I so much as set foot in the bar room my father would send me out again. There was cursing and swearing, they told jokes and broke glasses. They would come in quietly, proper gentlemen, with collars and ties, and order lamb or pork with a glass of white wine. After that the slivovitz would arrive, the tie would be unknotted, more slivovitz would arrive, sleeves would be rolled up. The men got redder and sweatier, and the more alcohol they tipped down themselves the more dirt came out. I used to spy on them through the serving hatch, like watching television on a forbidden channel. They drowned the music with their shouts and bawled their requests to the group. Every song had to be paid for, and they didn't always get what they wanted, but they had bundles of notes in their pockets to bribe the group with.'

'Did Ramiz play at your place too?'

'No, he was much too young, only a few months older than me. His father was the leader of our band, so I got to know him. Ramiz was still going to school and wanted to go on to the conservatoire. Not because he looked down on his father's group, although there was really something a bit shady about it.'

'What do you mean?'

'Oh, you should have heard the words of some of the songs: "We niggers, we layabouts, we can't let a handbag alone, or a woman, or a cow." That's what they sang, Ramo, Nezir, Indir, Sevdo and Sanija, the members of our band.'

'About themselves?'

'In the eyes of the customers, it was self-abasement, yes, so they laughed heartily and paid loads of money for it. But the customers were drunk, the gypsies were not. It was really a game, but I didn't understand that until later. As far as Ramiz was concerned, he refused point-blank to sing about thieving blacks. He only wanted to play for himself, "for the soul", as it's called in the bar room. The music is at its best when gypsies play for themselves, not for money. That was what Ramiz wanted, and he could do it, because his father, Ramo, had been selling his soul for so many years. That's why he was never angry with his father, but always a bit ashamed. He felt like a child who has been given a very expensive present.'

'How did you meet Ramiz? Did he come to your inn?'

'No, I went to the district where he lived. Not for his sake, I didn't even know him, I was simply curious. I didn't understand what was going on at home. Men in neat suits were singing that they were vagabonds and respectable customers were being dragged out legless. On my sixteenth birthday I went to the gypsy quarter on the sly. There were miserable alleyways, but also streets with big houses and highly-polished cars. Our band lived well. It was at that moment that I wondered who was making a fool of whom – the customers of the gypsies, or the gypsies of the customers. I was already on my way home when I heard someone call my name. It was Ramo, the violinist and *gusle* player. He had his son with him.'

'Ramiz?'

'Yes. He introduced us as if it were quite natural to find me in their district. I still think that was very decent of him, not to say: "What are you doing here?" But apart from that I wasn't thinking about him at all, because I was looking at Ramiz. Something clicked between us right away. From that day onwards, at least two and a half years ago, we went on meeting secretly. A friend of mine was in on the secret and always said I was with her when I was meeting Ramiz.'

'Why did it have to be so secret?'

'Because of my father and mother. His parents knew, and said nothing, because they knew that my parents, however much they valued the group, really despised gypsies. You feel those things. Apart from that, the war had begun and the request songs were different. The customers wanted to hear nationalist songs which had been forbidden before, but were soon being sung everywhere. Ramo had problems with that. He was tall, like Ramiz, but much broader and heavier, with longish, wavy hair and a terrific moustache. A very impressive man, who was capable of singing "I am a nigger" without turning a hair, but not "We Serbs are fighting...".'

'Did he have rows with your father?'

'Yes, now and then there was trouble, because it cost my father some customers. The kitchen was going downhill and if Ramo went on refusing to sing war songs, the bar business would get worse as well. My father was always thinking about money. For instance, if glasses were broken he made the customers pay by putting them on the bill. He began to make snide remarks and pester the band. Two of them, the guitarist and the accordion player, gave in and agreed to play nationalist songs in future. Result: trouble between them and Ramo. I think one of them told my father that I was going with Ramiz.'

'And then?'

'My father beat me, threw Ramo out and split the group. That was when we ran away, Ramiz and I. He left a farewell letter for his father and mother, but I got away in secret. I would really have liked to smash all their glasses on the floor, hundreds of wine and schnapps glasses in one go! But I thought: there will be time for that, I'll take my revenge later on. At three in the morning – it was dark outside, but warm – I escaped. Ramiz was waiting for me. I shall feel the kiss I got then for the rest of my life. For the first day we walked, but that was much too slow. We wanted to get to Hungary via Croatia. On the second day we got a lift in a bus which took us to Zagreb, but we were stopped on the way by paramilitaries, with a band round their heads. They cut off Ramiz's fingers.'

'Why?'

'So that he wouldn't forget how the Orthodox lot make the sign of the cross. There was a doctor on the bus who bandaged him and two others to whom they had done the same thing, as well as he could, with handkerchiefs and underwear, anything we had. It wasn't sterile, of course so all of them got feverish and had to get off the bus. Instead of getting out of the country we were stranded in a village where we had to wait for a doctor. An orderly cleaned the wounds, but the doctor had to sew them up. He came once a week. We didn't wait for him, we moved on, with pain-killers.'

'Mila!'

'Yes?'

'What a terrible story!'

'If only it was just a story! You, Josip, Haris and you, you never knew the real Ramiz. He used to laugh a lot, grumble a lot, have a joke with everyone. After the injury he changed. He began to realize that he would never be able to play again, not at his old level. And he was a perfectionist! The guitar was always near him, he was always playing. His hands were soft, but his fingers were always calloused, as if he were wearing ten thimbles. I did everything I could to help him, because I could see where it was going to end. He wanted to get me to safety, but he no longer cared about himself. Once he said it to my face: "Leave me, you go on."'

'But Mila, what did he himself want!'

'Surely you know that, or don't you? I was constantly afraid that he might do something stupid, jump off a mountain, run into a minefield. When he was quite silent I got more frightened than ever, so I used to start rows. At the same time I was trying to prepare myself. I had to be strong when it happened; someone would have to avenge him. And yet, when he suddenly ran down there I was horrified.'

'Do you think he deliberately…'

'Yes, he didn't run to the house to warn Josip and Haris. Oh well, yes, perhaps he did. Perhaps he had a bet with himself. If he arrived ahead of the men and could run there and back without being caught, he would accept his hand. Otherwise, it would all be over.'

'But they won't kill the boys, will they?'

'Look, Josip and Haris can give different names and say

126

they have a different religion, like Antonia. But Ramiz, with his dark skin and crippled hand, has no choice. Are you a Muslim, they will ask, and he will say yes, although Ramo played at any church festival where they wanted music.'

'But then of course the others will help him!'

'There's no "of course" about it. Not with the Chetnik militia. I know the mentality of those swine better than you do. Shall I tell you why? But you mustn't get angry with me. Promise me now.'

'Right,' said Aida anxiously.

'Don't get angry,' said Mila again. 'My own brothers are paras!'

There was a long silence.

Aida was glad it was dark. She felt the blood rising to her head now that the trash had come so close: the brothers of the girl beside her. In her confusion she could only say 'Oh!'

'I'm sorry,' said Mila. 'When the war began they were a waiter and a postman. Not exactly thrilling professions, and that's the way they looked, too. The older brother was already getting a belly on him. They watched television a lot, the Belgrade channel, where they went on every day about fame and blood brotherhood. Serbs were said to be indifferent citizens, but good, brave soldiers. That attracted my brothers. They used to show the corpses of murdered civilians, always Serb corpses.

'My brothers got excited. The elder grew a beard, the younger a moustache, and they started jogging again. I used to laugh at them, until I heard what they were doing at weekends. They went shooting, but not game: towns, hospitals and blocks of flats! "Do you think that's right?"

I wanted to scream at my parents, but I kept quiet. That was the year when Ramo and my father were quarrelling about the songs in the *kafana*, and I was terrified that Ramiz and I would be discovered.'

Aida sat up. 'How could you stand it?'

'What else could I do? It was dangerous to let myself go. I was already an outsider, quite different from my little sister, who always copied the others. After a year my brothers decided to become full-time Chetniks. That appealed to my father, he could boast about it to his customers. The first time they came home, both in battledress, they strutted through the town for hours with a "we're here to save you" look. That was grander than doling out letters or slivovitz. They began to make trouble, but my father played it down – just stress, he always said.

'The second time they were different, quieter, short-tempered. And the third time they snarled at my mother, and when she tried to stop them they grabbed her where a son doesn't grab his mother. My sister and I were frightened of them, but my father behaved as if he hadn't seen anything. He had no control over them. When they came home the *kafana* belonged to them. They got drunk, smashed up the furniture, and he sat on a bar stool and cursed his own sons. The war had turned them into savages and they couldn't stop.'

'Do you hate your brothers, Mila?'

'Yes, and my father and my mother and even my little sister. She's fifteen, like you, but what a little fool! Of course I know the television and the rest of the propaganda are responsible, but why are they so stupid, why do they believe everything they see on the box?'

Helplessly Aida put her arm round Mila's shoulders and when Mila hugged her Aida dared to hold her tighter, each trying to salve the other's grief.

Judging by the light outside, it was about nine when they woke up. They looked at each other in amazement and giggled at the way they were lying, their noses almost touching. Mila was the first to get up and do a few physical exercises, as usual. 'I'm wondering,' she said as she did her knee-bends, 'if Svetlana is giving milk again. If her udder is limp I'll leave her in peace and it will be easier to send her away when we leave the Gora.'

'Send her away?' murmured Aida.

'Yes, do you want to walk to Split with a goat and a dog on a lead? I think we should wait here a week, or ten days at the most. If the boys get away they will look for us here. But if they don't come we must move, Aida. In another month it will be autumn.'

Mila's self-assured tone annoyed Aida, as did her bending and stretching exercises. 'And when we're in Split, what then? We're suddenly going to be happy?'

Mila stopped her exercises and fell on her bed. 'You might, perhaps.'

'Fantastic, you're like Ramiz! He wanted to get you to safety, but he didn't care about himself. Spare yourself the trouble. I don't have to go to Split. I'll stay here and see what happens.'

Mila looked up curiously. 'You haven't half got a sharp tongue! I thought you were stuck up, but you can jaw and lash out. My brothers would be mad about you. I'm not going to Split to get you to safety, but to spend the winter there. If you want to do that alone on the

Gora, fine. Best of luck!' Mila stamped furiously out of the cave.

Aida heard the animals outside, bleating and barking. The sounds melted her anger and she would have liked to run after Mila. She had behaved unforgivably, but so had Mila, with her wise sayings and her gymnastics. If, like Aida, you had a natural tendency to blame yourself, strong people were hard to bear. And Mila was strong – and older.

Aida spread her fingers and combed through her hair, which was getting more and more matted. She looked at her damaged nails. the scratches on her hands and arms and examined her nose, which was no longer quite so swollen. On the way out she saw the boys' shaving mirror and walked quickly past it.

Mila was sitting between the goat and the dog, stroking them in turns.

'Shall we let Napoleon run free?' asked Aida.

'He would run straight down to the village.'

'How is Svetlana? Are you going to milk her or not?'

'I've decided not to.'

'But if we go away,' Aida wondered aloud, 'what's to become of the animals? Can a goat live in the snow? And Napoleon, what will he eat?'

'I don't know,' said Mila. 'They will either return to the wild or die. But I can't kill them, and I can't take them along either.'

'Can't we wait longer? A month, instead of only ten days?'

'No. By then it will be October and we'll be in trouble ourselves. If the boys are not back in a week it means that they've probably been taken to a camp. Then it could be months.'

Aida turned pale. In her mind's eye she could see Haris going down the Gora just ahead of her, with curls that bounced at every step, carrying a shovel. 'Are you angry?' she had asked him. And he had said, 'No, I'm afraid.'

'But Mila,' she said desperately, 'if they come back in two weeks and miss us, we will have lost each other!'

'So we must leave them a letter. There's next to no chance of anyone else finding it up here.'

'What about the chance of their finding it?'

'That's reading the coffee grounds. Ramiz's mother sometimes did it with coffee, reading the future in the grounds.'

'Do you believe in it?' asked Aida

Mila smiled. 'Oh, she didn't sit there in a long dress gazing into a crystal ball. It just happened at the table after a meal, when we were drinking coffee. She would look at the grounds and foretell the future. Usually vaguely, you didn't learn anything, but it was very comfortable and friendly. I felt more at home with Ramiz's family than with my own father and mother.

'My parents were so shut-in. "Home-made", "absolutely natural", 'genuine"; the purity of those menus made you quite dizzy. But the purity was all pretence, just as it was with the orchestra. My father boasted that he had genuine gypsies playing for him – home-made, absolutely natural. But when his daughter fell in love with a genuine gypsy he was just genuinely furious.'

# Chapter 15

*Dear boys,*
*We've waited ten days for you, but now we have to leave the*
*Gora. We have let Napoleon and Svetlana go, there was*
*nothing else to do. We hope the animals will manage in the cold.*
*We dismantled our kitchen because we thought it was better to*
*remove all traces outside the cave. But the pots and cutlery are*
*all there, you'll find them in one of the beds. We're going to*
*walk to Split. If we get there we shall ask for you every day at*
*the market down by the harbour, and at the Iron Gate, which*
*is the west gate of the town. If there's a hotel there we'll enquire*
*at the reception. And if there's no hotel we'll ask the nearest*
*shopkeepers to help us. That way we'll hope to meet up again.*
*There is still enough food, you will be able to manage for a while*
*if you can't follow us immediately. There are tins here, too.*
*Don't worry about us. There has been no more shooting in the*
*valleys round the Gora for a week now and the road is fairly*
*safe. We're leaving with as much food as possible, and two*
*blankets. And the torch. Sorry. Both of us very much hope that*
*you will read this letter. Best of luck for the trip to the coast, and*
*hope to see you soon.*

*Love, Mila and Aida*

The letter lay on the bedclothes, beside the food stores,
among the kitchen cutlery, under the shaving mirror and
beside the oil lamp. At Aida's suggestion they had copied
it four times and spread it around like pamphlets, so that
if the boys came they were certain to find it.

Calling them 'dear boys' had been Mila's idea. If no
names were named it didn't matter which of the boys
read the letter. So it was not the heartfelt letter that she

had been composing for days in her mind, but a sober, sensible account. As Mila had written nothing about Ramiz, Aida did not ask after Haris, and for the same reason they had not mentioned Josip.

After inspecting the cave for the last time they were faced with the most difficult part of their departure. In the letter they had written about it in the past, as if the job was already done, but it was still ahead of them. In the morning Mila had untied the dog and the goat, but nothing had happened. They had continued to look at her with undiminished friendliness. Aida had shouted 'Go away!' and 'Shoo!' without much conviction, but that had not helped either. The animals, by now fairly experienced, simply stayed put.

Aida and Mila packed up, sighing. They took as many light things as possible and only a couple of tins, because the water alone, in two-litre plastic bottles, made their rucksacks heavy. They looked out at intervals as they packed, but the animals were still there. The goat was grazing peacefully and Napoleon was lying in the shadow of a tree, his head on his paws. He was not altogether calm as they could see from his twitching tail.

'What shall we do now?' asked Aida.

'I don't know,' said Mila. 'Perhaps just run off on the sly.'

'Can we really not take them with us? Then if we pass through a village where someone is still living we could leave them there.'

'And what if we don't pass through a village?' asked Mila somewhat desperately. 'What if we have to hide on the way and one starts bleating and the other barking?'

'All right then, run off on the sly.'

Unhappily they looked from the dog to the goat and then at each other. They were as nervous as if they were waiting for the starting-pistol before a race. Silently they gave each other a nod and suddenly began to run.

They rushed out of the cave, up the Gora, towards the northern slope, not daring to look round. They ran as fast as they could and sat down panting where the path began. Loud barking made them jump. Napoleon stood above them, his tongue hanging out, and although he was wagging his tail he was clearly suspicious.

Aida began to laugh wildly. 'Shall I get the rope?'

'No, then Svetlana will come too. We must go down and that's that.'

With the dog at their heels they began the climb down to the village and the road. It was not pleasant to see Brodište coming closer step by step. The more they could see, the sharper their memories became, but they had to get down the mountain somehow, and the mines made the southern slope too dangerous.

'What do you think?' said Mila, when they reached the level of the cemetery. 'Shall we, or better not?'

'Quickly,' said Aida.

They found the meagre cross and were relieved that no one had taken it away. Mila laid two wrinkled apples on the grave, Aida a few flowers, and the same for the neighbouring grave. These simple actions awakened so many emotions that they did not notice the dog running off.

'Where is Napoleon?' asked Aida.

Mila frowned. They stared across at Antonia's house, which drew them like a magnet.

'We're quite crazy,' said Mila. 'We try to escape from

135

the dog and as soon as he leaves us, we run after him.' All the same, Mila seemed unable to control her own movements. Together they ran to the house, where they saw Napoleon rushing distractedly to and fro. The glass in the door was broken and the curtains, furniture and household goods inside were in chaos: all torn, burned or smashed.

'What was the point of that?' cried Aida.

Mila turned pale. 'They were probably looking for slivovitz. When the boys get away I hope they don't have to see this! Aida, I want to go!'

But Aida was looking through the broken window in Antonia's room and managed with some difficulty to pull out a photograph. 'For Josip,' she said, pushing the frame into her rucksack. Then they ran from the terrace and the ghost village.

Napoleon stayed behind. Now and then they heard him yelping softly in the distance.

For hours they walked side by side without a word, thinking of the old dog who had stayed alone in the village and thus condemned himself to death. He would drink from the stream. And they thought of the goat, which continued to walk round in circles as if she were still tied up, and of the devastation in the house, the grave that no one had visited, and of their letter on the mountain. They thought until they were so exhausted and limp from the heat that they stopped thinking and simply walked. They passed by Izvor, Brezik and Turovi, villages like Brodište where no one lived – not even old women with ugly dogs.

At the hottest hour of the day they stopped to drink

136

and rest. Aida pulled off her shoes and rubbed her painful toes.

'Already?' said Mila, surprised.

'My shoes are getting too small for me. I'm still growing, is that so strange?'

'No, of course not, sorry. I sometimes forget that you are fifteen. I went on growing until I was seventeen, then I stopped. Are your father and mother tall?'

'My father was tall, I think. He died in a skiing accident and I never really knew him. My mother is a bit shorter than I am, I've already outgrown her.'

'Should we cut out the toecaps, do you think?'

'No, are you kidding? It's all right.' Aida put her shoes on again hastily. They might cramp her big toes a bit, but they fitted well.

'But we've got to walk for days,' said Mila. 'And I don't dare to hope that the Blues will give us a lift. This area is an absolute desert.'

Aida nodded thoughtfully. Pedro had not returned either. As soon as fighting broke out the traffic was diverted. She sighed as she looked at her shoes, remembering her mother's excitement when she had brought them home. The siege of Tuz and the refugees in the town meant that certain articles, such as shoes, had become almost unobtainable. The shoes were not new, either, but second-hand, from someone with even longer toes.

'Will you be all right?' asked Mila.

Aida stood up. 'Yes, I'm fine,' she said bravely. The sooner they got to a safer area, the better for them. After they had hoisted their rucksacks on their backs they set off again towards the south, walking on the verge to get as much shade as possible from the trees. Their shadows followed them, merging every few metres with the shadow of a leafy tree. To save time they ate as they walked: currants, biscuits, crackers, apples and lumps of sugar.

The sun was already setting when they heard the sound of an engine on the empty road behind them. Instinctively they ducked down on the verge. A white car appeared. 'Yes or no?' asked Mila. They would have to decide in three seconds. 'No,' said Aida, 'or...yes!'

They jumped from the shadow of the trees on to the sun-drenched asphalt. The white station wagon stopped. It was not a UN vehicle.

Someone stepped out on the left-hand side and stared at them over the roof. 'Where the hell did you spring from?'

They did not answer. Aida was cursing her toes which would prevent her from running away, and Mila got out her penknife.

The man slumped back into the car, where a second man was sitting. The girls could hear them speaking English. The second man stared at the girls curiously through the open window and suddenly he was holding a camera and taking pictures of them. Aida and Mila shrieked.

'Calm down,' said the first man, 'he's a photographer, I'm an interpreter, we wouldn't hurt a fly, him and me. Where do you two come from?'

'From Brodište,' said Mila, without putting her knife away. 'Stop taking photographs. Tell him to stop at once!'

The interpreter tapped the photographer on the shoulder and announced after a moment, 'It's all right, he's stopping.'

'And how long is it going to take him?' Mila shouted, because the photographer was still snapping. She struck out angrily at the lens. That did the trick. The man withdrew his head and stowed away the camera.

'Can we give you a lift?' asked the interpreter helpfully. 'I assume you want to get away from here?'

Mila hesitated. She had noticed that Aida was moving her feet to and fro restlessly, like someone who had wet herself. But she didn't like the look of the interpreter. He had a narrow, insolent face and unfriendly eyes. It was the face of a man who makes himself useful only when there is something in it for him. 'Have you got identity cards?'

'Why not?' said the interpreter sarcastically. He scratched his stubble and spoke to the photographer, who showed his press pass.

'Does the name mean anything to you?' asked Mila, nudging Aida. Neither name nor pass was important, she was only trying to get an impression of the photographer and to involve Aida. Her English was poor, but perhaps Aida could ask some questions.

'Listen,' said the interpreter, 'here you are, roaming like two wood nymphs through an area from which only the moles have not yet escaped! Do we have to prove our identity to get you evacuated?' With an exaggerated gesture he looked at his watch.

'Just a moment,' said the photographer, looking at the girls. 'I'm leaving Bosnia. You too? Have you got passports?'

They shook their heads despondently.

'Oh, leave it,' said the photographer. 'We'll see how it goes. My name's Jim. Coming along?'

Aida's toes decided it. The girls put their rucksacks in the luggage space and sat on the back seat. The interpreter drove off, accelerating so hard on each gear change that the vehicle leapt forward. The tree-tops rushed past. The sound reminded Mila of the whirring of the automatic camera. Why had the Englishman taken photographs of them? 'Wood nymphs', the interpreter had called them. With their sun-browned faces, unkempt hair and dirty, torn clothes, they probably looked pretty wild.

Mila saw that Aida had taken off her shoes and was stretching her toes. From time to time she replied to a question from the Englishman, who had begun a conversation. He was a freelance war photographer, working for papers and journals all over the world, and he loved stress, he said.

The road began to climb and the interpreter had to change down to third and then second gear. 'Shut the windows,' he ordered, 'and duck if anything goes wrong. When we're through here we come into a Croat-held area.'

Mila bit her lip. This was something she and Aida had not yet discussed. She waited in vain for the Englishman to stop talking so that she could say something. It was not until they passed a wrecked tanker, hanging like a gigantic seesaw with its front wheels over a cliff, that he stopped for a moment.

At once Mila clutched Aida's arm. 'From now on my name is Greta. Get it? Don't forget, will you?'

'What a silly name,' said Aida. 'Can't you think of something else?'

'What's wrong with Greta? Don't get it wrong, remember. And take care with the men.'

'Which men?'

'These...'

# Chapter 16

They came over the mountain unscathed. The interpreter, who knew this stretch well, had taken a gravel road along the ravine to pass unnoticed through the Serbian-occupied area. The landscape became increasingly barren. Before them stretched the melancholy karst range, where the bushes and grass had either been cut down or grazed or washed away by the rain which was constantly pouring down the mountains. Only where the earth was level was the fruitful soil still held together by tree roots.

'Golo,' said the interpreter, nodding his head towards the town among the barren mountains. While they were still looking at the houses, gardens and fields, they were stopped. Suddenly two soldiers were standing in the road. With their rifle butts they directed the vehicle to a road-block some thirty metres ahead.

Mila and Aida froze. 'Don't be frightened,' said the interpreter, 'I'll fix it with the men.'

At the road-block were two men from the HVO, the Bosnian-Croat Defence Council. 'Hi, Ante!' So they must know the interpreter. 'Got your daughters with you?'

'These girls come from Brodište.' The interpreter looked round at them. 'Tell the men your names.'

'Aida,' said Aida.

'Greta,' said Mila.

'Will that do?' asked Ante. 'They are going to register at an office in Croatia.'

One of the men laughed. 'Make sure they have pleasant memories of you, Ante.'

They scarcely glanced at Jim's press pass.

'That's done,' said Ante, letting the station wagon roll down the mountainside. Golo, where there were already some lighted windows, was a town with pergolas, terraces and window-boxes. Aida and Mila looked in astonishment at the undamaged houses.

'It's too late to drive any further,' they heard the interpreter tell the photographer. 'Shall we get something to eat?'

They jumped when Ante turned to them. 'You're invited too! I have relations here.'

Mila grasped Aida's hand and pinched it in warning. 'We have too,' she said. 'Well, no, not relations, but friends. We're going to see them.'

The interpreter's face darkened. 'Oh no, you're not going to leave Jim and me in the lurch after that long drive?'

'Of course not,' said Mila. 'Tell us where you're going to spend the night and we'll come and see you in the morning. I think we'll be staying on a bit.' She could see his angry eyes in the rear mirror.

'Right, tell me where to put you down. I know every street here. Every one!'

'Put us down at the corner. The last bit is so awkward. You won't be able to turn.'

Both Aida, who had no idea what was going on, and the Englishman, who had not understood a word, looked up in surprise when they stopped. The interpreter walked round the car and took out their rucksacks.

Mila thanked them for the lift and put out her hand politely. The interpreter saw it but did not take it. 'Best wishes to your friends,' he said, jumping in behind the wheel again. Even the engine sounded furious as he accelerated and drove away.

'Why did you say that?' Aida asked.

Mila sighed. 'Even someone with blisters on their feet should keep her wits about her,' she said. 'What did you think of the interpreter?'

'A bit slimy, perhaps.'

'A bit much!' said Mila.

'Yes but, Mila, what are we going to do now?'

'My name is Greta, don't get it wrong. Mila is as Serbian as all get out!'

'But you're not a nationalist. You go around with a gypsy, you…'

'Am I supposed to hang a placard on my chest saying: "I am a Serb, but a good one"? Do you think the Croats here will be impressed by a girl who loves a gypsy? They look down on gypsies here as much as they do in Serbia! But even if things were different I don't want to show Ramiz off as my little in-house orchestra. Ramiz was my boyfriend!'

Their appearance and their hectic whispers were attracting attention. Passers-by looked round curiously or even walked slowly to hear what they were saying. Feeling lost, they picked up their rucksacks and turned into one side street, then another, then another, until they came to a dead end on a path that led into a garden behind a house and a brick garage. Aida took a sip of water and leaned against the hedge.

'Right, I admit that he was slimy, but now we're in a real jam. It was probably only another two hours to the coast and he could just have driven on.'

'Yes,' said Mila, 'but he didn't. He wanted to take us

for dinner, and for pudding, too.'

'And the other one,' said Aida, trying to remember the photographer talking about his work in the car, 'did he want that too?'

'I don't know,' said Mila. 'In my opinion he was in love with himself. A cowboy with a camera. Do you think you'll be able to walk tomorrow?'

'If you cut the toecaps off.'

Mila turned to the hedge and pushed aside the leathery leaves of the laurel bushes. Behind them lay an enclosed garden with dense, leafy shrubs. 'As long as they haven't got a dog, I could sleep here.'

'What about the people?' asked Aida. 'If they come into the garden they'll call the police.'

'Who walks about in the garden at night? There is an outside light on the left side of the house where their terrace is. We'll wait until they've gone to bed, then we'll creep into the garden. All right?'

Aida did not answer. She nibbled biscuits and crackers, sucked sugar lumps and slurped down a tin of beans because they had forgotten the cutlery. She was beginning to feel sick, but also drowsy, and when Mila said they could go into the garden now, she could have slept on park benches, on the street itself, and even on roof tiles. 'I'll wait here,' she murmured.

'No, you'll come with me,' said Mila, pulling her up. Between the laurel hedge and the garage wall there was a gap which allowed them to slip into the garden. They stood still, listening anxiously. 'No dog!' said Mila with relief, and suddenly remembered Napoleon who had so sadly stayed behind.

'I wonder if he's still sitting on the steps behind the

house,' said Aida.

More and more often they found themselves quite independently thinking the same thoughts, which cut down their conversations.

'He must be, where else?' Mila had unpacked the blankets and spread them on the ground between three shrubs. They lay down, sighing, breathing in the vanilla scent of the laurel hedge and the spicy aroma of the cedars. 'I can smell the sea, can you? We used to go to the seaside every year, and when we were almost there I would put my head out of the car to smell the laurels, the lavender and the eucalyptus trees. Oh, the holidays smelled so wonderful!'

Aida rolled herself up in a blanket and thought of her own holidays. They used to go to the mountains in Slovenia or Macedonia, as if her mother were always looking for her father.

'What are you thinking about?' asked Mila.

'The mountains. My mother and I used to have our holidays in the mountains.'

Satisfied with the brief reply, Mila put her arm round Aida and they fell into an exhausted sleep.

There was a dog, after all! Very early the next morning he stuck his nose through the leaves of the bushes and announced the girls to the people of the house. Mila and Aida jumped up. Stiff as they were, they rolled up their blankets in a flash. 'My shoes!' moaned Aida.

The barking turned into a growl, until a fat man appeared and calmed the dog down. 'What have we here? Who are you?'

'We're on our way to Split,' said Mila, as if that

explained everything.

'We've come from Brodište,' Aida added.

'Aha!' said the man. 'Yes, well, of course you had to cross my garden, it's obvious.' He turned to the house and called, 'Greta! Greta, come here a minute?'

A woman in a dressing-gown came running out. Her mouth opened as she stared at the girls and their packs and blankets.

'They slept here,' her husband explained. 'They're on their way from Brodište to Split.'

'My God,' said the woman, 'can it be true? Where are your parents? Stayed behind? Over there? Oh, Vinko, what's to become of this country if people are forced to sle p in back gardens? Tell me, what are your names?'

'Aida,' said Aida.

'Greta,' said Mila hesitantly.

'Oh, like me, did you hear that, Vinko? Wouldn't you like to freshen up a bit? Can I wash anything for you? You can't go to Split like that, you look like a couple of savages! Come on!'

She walked ahead of the girls to the open terrace door, followed by the man and the dog. It was clear who wore the trousers in this house.


Soon afterwards Aida and Mila were sitting in the bathtub. In the absence of bath salts, Greta had poured shampoo into the water and stirred it thoroughly. 'You must be properly soaked,' she said. 'And your clothes, too. Don't hurry, take all the time you need.'

They stared at the door through which the woman had vanished with their clothes.

'What a turn-up,' said Mila. 'I don't think I've been

148

put in the bathtub like this since I was four years old!'

'I wouldn't mind being four again.' Aida drew a breath and blew it out under water. 'I'm a motorboat, brrrm!'

'The door,' said Mila.

'What about the door?'

'I'm going to shut it.' A dripping Mila walked over to the bathroom door and turned the key. 'There!'

Aida laughed. She put back her head, closed her eyes and relaxed. 'I'm not going to walk to Split,' she said suddenly. 'I'm going to spend the rest of my life in the bath.'

Mila too closed her eyes.

It was very quiet. They could hear nothing but the shampoo bubbles bursting. The water cooled down slowly.

'About another sixty years,' said Mila.

'What?'

'For you to sit in the bath. Seventy, if you live till you're very old.'

'So have I got to come to Split?'

Mila clasped Aida's legs comfortingly between her knees. 'It's the only place in the world where we may find them again.'

'Yes.'

At last they washed their hair properly and scrubbed each other's dirty backs. Then they rinsed off the foam and wrapped themselves in towels.

'I wish I had your figure,' said Mila. 'I'm so short and plump, and I've got one of those awful female behinds!'

'No, you're not fat at all. You're just muscular, you know.'

'Yes, yes, you should see my mother, she's even more

149

muscular! Eighty kilos and round as a barrel. What's your mother like, Aida?'

'Tall, slim, perhaps a bit thin, with light blonde hair like me. She worked in the library in Tuz. When I'm in Split I'm going to look for her. She…'

Mila pursed her lips. 'Shush, I know all about it from Haris. I'm going to help you, okay?'

Lost in thought, they sat on the edge of the bath for some time, waiting. The woman had gone through their rucksacks unasked and taken their spare clothes with her. They had nothing but towels. Suddenly the door handle rattled.

'May I come in?' asked Greta, her arms full of clothes again. 'My daughters left home years ago, but I thought I could find something for you. I got these from the attic. They're old, but clean. See if they fit. I've put the other things to soak.'

One came down in a dress, the other in training pants and t-shirt. The woman, who in many ways reminded them of Antonia, had laid the table. 'It's difficult to get meat,' she said, 'but this is good soil and we have plenty of fruit and vegetables.' She pushed a dish of melon slices in front of them and invited them to take bread, tomatoes, paprikas and fresh olives as well.

'Do you like olives, Greta?'

Aida nudged Mila, who pulled herself together quickly and said 'Yes'. Vinko had disappeared behind a newspaper. *Serbia swallowing up Balkans*, was one of the headlines.

Sighing, the older Greta poured tea. With a glance at the paper she said, 'This war is too much for me.

150

Brodište, Izvor, Turovi – last year they all still belonged to us. But the Chetniks are advancing all the time. I'm sometimes even afraid for Golo. Where shall we go if they come? I believe we Bosnian Croats would do well to join up with Croatia. That would make us stronger.'

Mila stared, embarrassed, at the well-scraped melon rind. 'Where would that leave Aida?' she ventured at last.

The woman looked searchingly at the pretty, blonde girl, who had stopped eating. 'Are you a Muslim?' she asked.

Aida wanted to say no, but then, what was she? A descendant of the Bogomils? Why did she have a name that indicated a religion she had never believed in?

It was Tito, the atheist, for goodness sake, whom she had to thank for her name! If you looked at Yugoslavia as a chorus of ten races, two were singing too loud: Serbia and Croatia. In order to pin them down, Tito gave the Yugoslavs with Muslim backgrounds a Muslim nationality. It was as simple and foolish as that. Aida shook back her wet hair and said, 'I'm a Bosnian!'

The woman smiled. 'Of course, child, of course. We were all that once, Vinko, Greta, you and I. But there is no more Bosnia-Herzegovina.'

But there's still me, thought Aida.

The fat man lowered his paper. 'Please stop talking politics. Women don't know anything about it.' He gave them a wicked wink.

'Oh, of course, men do!' said Greta. 'They've proved over the last four years that they know far more about it.' She wasn't being serious either, because she giggled and embarrassed the girls a little when she stroked Vinko's almost bald head. 'My Vinko is not as bad as he makes

151

out. He will take you to Split.'

They looked up, surprised.

'I'm a fishmonger. I drive regularly to Split for fresh supplies. The stretch to the Bosnian–Croatian frontier is the worst, because there are riff-raff there who would put a gun to your head for nothing at all. I advise you not to walk there. I haven't got an armoured car, of course, and they might stop me, too, but...'

'He can tell good stories,' said Greta. 'You should do that, go with Vinko. Have you got relations in Split?'

'Friends,' said Mila. 'We've arranged to meet friends there.' Her eyes met Aida's.

# Chapter 17

'Good morning,' came a low voice. Rade looked up from the ladies' shoes for which he was making new heels. The doors of his workshop were always wide open in summertime so that he could see the sea and the palm trees. 'Yes?' he asked eagerly, because he was a man who loved a chat. But he frowned when he saw the boys from yesterday afternoon. 'No,' he said, before they had asked him anything. 'They haven't been here today either.'

The boys wandered off and he watched them walking despondently across the busy market square. He hammered harder to work off his regret over his own gruffness.

The door to the living-room opened suddenly. 'Papa!' cried his daughter. 'Were the boys here again?'

'Yes, for the third time, I think.'

'And what did you say?'

'I told them the truth, what else? In other words: no!'

'But they were here, Papa, just now! Two girls, Mama says. You were in the back and she was watching the workshop for you.'

'Why didn't she tell me?'

'She was going to, but you had a customer and you started talking. So she told me. Where have the boys gone?'

'Across the square. You'll never find them.'

But his daughter ran out of the workshop and vanished in the crowded square. Her father had started on another pair of shoes by the time she came back, looking disappointed.

'They've gone. Now they've missed each other,

because you always have to chat to everyone!'

Rado gave her an angry look. 'There are thirty thousand Bosnians here, and they've all lost somebody. Am I supposed to sit in front of my shop like a marriage broker? I sit here to earn my bread. And your pocket money, don't forget that.'

'Then I'll telephone out of my pocket money,' said the girl, going through the inner door to the telephone in the hall.

The motor camp where Mila and Aida were living was called 'Jadran'. They had spent a week with Greta and Vinko in Golo, until the fishmonger had given them a lift to Split. They had registered formally as Greta Muk from Brodište and Aida Osmić from Tuz, and they had been formally allocated to two reception centres.

'But we belong together!' Mila protested.

The man in the refugee office had smiled feebly and said that Bosnian Muslims and Bosnian Croats were accommodated separately. 'But what if we were married?' Mila tried again. 'What if she was my husband?'

'Ah, if,' said the man, sighing, and handed them the address of the motor camp site. 'Try there,' he advised them. 'They are private owners, they don't have as many regulations as we do.'

So Aida and Mila had ended up in a caravan which they had to share with another, rather careworn, woman. The caravan stood on a motor camp site in which there was not a single car to be seen – nor any campers, for that matter. The only people living there were refugees, in identical, small caravans. Fortunately the woman went off in the morning and did not return until late afternoon, so that they could imagine themselves to be on holiday. The surroundings helped. Pine trees filtered the sunlight and made patterns on the ground – always sharp and changing.

The camp administration had given them swimsuits, and they had gone off to bathe on their third day in Jadran. The beach was filthy, the bay was silted up and because there were no tourists but only Bosnian refugees, it was never dredged.

They brushed the salt from their shoulders and decided to wash the mud off later. Idly they stretched out on the scratchy, straw-dry floor of the wood.

'Greta, Aida!'

They sat up and saw Ana, the woman from the camp administration, walking over to them. She squatted beside them. 'I've just had an odd telephone call.'

'Who from?' asked Mila and Aida at the same time.

'From a girl in Split. She says her father is a shoemaker, and some boys called to ask after you.'

'On the market place? By the harbour?' asked Aida.

'Yes,' said Ana, 'that would be right, then?'

'When? How many boys?' asked Mila. She was sitting bolt upright, her eyes staring.

'Today... I suppose there were two boys. The girl said something about "a couple". Here's her telephone number, or have you got it already?'

Mila did not answer. She was as white as chalk. Aida did not answer either: she was afraid that Mila might faint and wished Ana would go away. It was obvious now that in spite of her constant assertions, Mila was in no way

155

reconciled to the fate of her friend Ramiz. It had been bravado, or superstition: if I hope he's alive, he's dead; if I think he's dead, he's alive. Aida realized in a flash how her friend's mind had been working.

When Ana had gone Mila began to cry. At last the tears which she had been holding back all this time came flooding out. She sobbed so noisily that Aida tugged her into the caravan out of sight and hearing of their neighbours.

'There may be three of them after all. "A couple" is just something you say, but it could just as well mean three. And even if there are two of them, one of those may be Ramiz.' But however hard she tried, it did no good. Mila lay face down and sobbed. In the end Aida could only hope that their companion would stay away.

But just that afternoon she came back earlier than usual. 'What's wrong?' she asked.

Aida shrugged her shoulders. It was not something that could be explained in a few words. The woman fetched aspirin tablets and dissolved them in water. 'Here, give her this, she's gone to pieces. And stay with her. You're friends, aren't you?'

'Yes,' said Aida.

When Mila had calmed down a little, Aida took her notebook, a ball-point and some small change. 'I'll go and telephone,' she whispered. 'You stay where you are, okay?'

Their fellow occupant cleared her throat and when Aida turned she saw the woman whose presence they found so obtrusive, standing in the middle of the caravan. 'I don't know what's wrong,' she said, 'but shall I keep an eye on her?'

'Fine,' said Aida, blushing, and jumped down over the little steps. No one stopped her, no one asked questions, and yet it seemed to her that all the people sitting on deckchairs in this summer weather were watching her curiously. Some of them had been living here for years and had porches or extra tents in front of their caravans. Under these were rugs and cushions, and even pots of plants.

Aida leafed through her notebook. In two days Mila and she had enquired after the boys at a baker's shop, three hotels, a newspaper kiosk, a shoemaker's shop and an ice-cream parlour. And each time they had left their names and telephone number. What had happened?

She went to the office beside the camp barrier. The notice in the window read 'Tax-free shop', but the cigarettes and drinks which had once been sold there had been replaced by calculators, computers and telephones.

'Ana, may I telephone?'

'To the shoemaker?'

Aida nodded.

Ana opened the half door so that Aida could go through the counter into the office. 'It's difficult. The lines are overloaded – by UNPROFOR again, if you ask me. But you can try.'

Aida was glad that Ana gave her a little privacy by going on with her own work. She dialled the number nervously. Engaged. Under the blouse which she had pulled on hastily over her swimsuit she felt the sweat running down her back. She must get a connection! She tried again, and this time she got through.

'Hallo, yes?' said a woman's voice.

'Good morning, I'm Aida. Can I talk to your

daughter?'

'Which one? I've got three.'

'Oh, well, the one who rang me up, me and Greta.'

'Just a minute, I don't really understand.'

There was silence for some minutes, until suddenly a girl's voice shouted, 'Hallo, I'm Marija.'

Aida swallowed. 'Aida here. Did you call us? We came to your father's workshop and asked after three boys.'

'Oh yes, I'm glad you've rung! Sorry it went wrong. You were talking to my mother.'

'That's possible,' said Aida nervously.

'Sorry,' said the girl again, 'but my mother knows nothing about it and my father wasn't there at that moment. That's why.'

'Did they come?' asked Aida desperately.

'Yes, three times in all!'

'How many of them?' asked Aida. The trickle of sweat down her back had become a stream, and her head was ready to burst.

'Two,' said Marija. 'Always two.'

'How did they look?'

'Tired and a bit dirty.'

'That's not what I mean! Describe them, or did they give their names?'

'No, they always said they would come back. I haven't got an address, either.'

'What did they look like then? Dark?'

'Oh yes, they were very brown! One of them was tall, with smooth, blonde hair and the other had black curls.'

Now that Aida knew, the tension faded. 'Thanks,' she said, feeling suddenly quite exhausted. 'When they come back, please would you tell them that we're in Jadran?

And that they should telephone us? You've got our number.'

'Yes, right,' said the girl.

'And thank you again!' Aida called hastily, but the girl had already hung up.

'Well, any the wiser?' asked Ana casually.

'Yes, a little,' said Aida, leaving the office quickly. She didn't want to talk to anyone. First she had to digest for herself the news that Josip and Haris had come alone, but she had scarcely succeeded by the time she reached the caravan. What was she to tell Mila? She would have preferred to put it off, but the eyes of the people on their deckchairs drove her inside.

'Did you phone?' asked Mila.

'Yes, I talked to the girl.' Aida looked with painful sympathy at her friend, who was lying, small and vulnerable, on the bed.

'There were two of them, no Ramiz, right?'

'Oh, Mila, I'm so sorry!' Aida leaned over the bed to put her arms round Mila. Perhaps Ramiz had come with them and was in hospital, or still imprisoned. Her imagination supplied explanations, which she put forward hesitantly.

But Mila only shook her head. She became extraordinarily calm. 'I knew,' she whispered. 'I always knew. Would you lie beside me for a while?'

Aida stretched out on the bed and they lay there for a long time, still sticky and covered with salt from their swim.

Suddenly Mila asked, 'Are you keen on Haris, Aida?'

'Me on Haris? Why?'

'You were always going to the *stećci*, weren't you? You stayed away for hours. Did you never… well, you know?'

'No,' said Aida. 'We quarrelled! About religion and history. I didn't want to quarrel, it just happened, especially when he talked about the Bogomils.'

'Really?' asked Mila.

'Do you know what he said the Bogomils believed? That the earth was the creation of Satan, the first son of God. It was a mistake, and that was why God sent his second son to help human beings.'

'There's something in that,' said Mila.

'There's nothing in it. It's wrong. How can a good God have a son like Satan?'

'A bad mother, perhaps,' said Mila with a cynical laugh. 'Many religions see the sinful woman as the explanation for everything.'

It was dusk, and in the other half of the caravan they heard something drop. There was the strange, thin woman, who had probably been listening to everything.

'What did you arrange with the shoemaker's daughter?'

'If the boys come back, she'll give them our telephone number here in Jadran. They have already been three times, but without leaving an address or telephone number. Why did you ask about Haris – if I was in love with him and all that?'

'Oh, I thought that though I've lost someone, you might be getting someone back. I know it's nonsense, but I thought at least there might be something to be thankful for.'

'Mila, we're both getting someone back! The boys are

our friends.'

'That's true. Our friends,' said Mila.

# Chapter 18

For a week now Josip and Haris had been sleeping in a wood bordering the beach. After the last bather had gone home they washed in the showers on the concrete floor and walked into the wood to eat their umpteenth packet of crackers or tin of beans. Supplies were running low and so were their reserves. Josip was beginning to grumble at Haris's stubbornness. 'We ought to register,' he said. 'I'm breaking my back on these stones!' He slapped his hand on the rocky ground on which their blankets lay.

'And then you think you'll get a hotel bed right away? The town is overflowing with refugees. Every pension, every camp site is stuffed with us!'

'We ought to try,' said Josip.

'Try what?' asked Haris. 'Why should I need a passport in a country I've always lived in? People from here used to go to Sarajevo to shop or visit museums, and we went to the beach for a day. But suddenly it's abroad! We speak the same language, but we're suddenly foreigners. I have to prove who I am!'

Josip sighed. 'It's a real pain, but what can I do about it? My back hurts.'

'Listen,' said Haris, lying down on the blanket, 'I'll tell you a fairy story.'

Josip was going to run off in a huff but Haris held him back. 'A short story. Once upon a time there was a beautiful country where different kinds of people lived. Sometimes things went well, sometimes badly. That's human beings for you. But even if they sometimes quarrelled, they always made it up again, to enjoy the countryside, drink a glass of slivovitz or eat a plate of djuveć. One day a bunch of madmen arrived who wanted to have all the slivovitz, all the djuveć and all the countryside. They knew it would not be easy and so they became soldiers. They became sergeants, lieutenants, captains, colonels, very powerful! And after that they took over the army, with everything that could ride, fly or fire! The people were scared to death, and yet, when they were shot at, instead of blaming the madmen they blamed their neighbours. They didn't understand the madmen, but their neighbours were familiar, they had often quarrelled with them – and after all, you have to blame someone when the bullets are flying round your ears. In the row that broke out then wise men came from the east and west. They took a quick look round and said, "Everyone here is mad, this is a country of madmen! We must separate them!" And they altered the frontiers, and did it again, and again, and again, until no one dared to draw a map of Yugoslavia.'

'Fine,' said Josip, 'you can tell that to your children later, but I don't need stories. Man, what I need is a bed!' He stood up painfully and wandered down the beach. He was one metre ninety tall and when he was troubled and had no proper bed, his back played up. He went to the water-line and allowed the luke-warm water to run to and fro over his feet. Had this water – ebbing and flowing for ever – touched Aida too?

At first he had been shocked by the unnatural silence on the Gora, then he had seen the letters. 'Dear boys' five times over. He and Haris had hugged each other with relief.

The girls had gone to Split, but they would meet again

on the market square or by the Iron Gate. Josip walked further into the water, careless of the salt rings on his trouser legs. He looked like a tramp, but what did that matter? Who would notice?

'Josha!' Haris waded through the water until he was standing next to Josip. 'We'll get ourselves passes tomorrow, okay?'

'Right,' said Josip. And in their soaking wet trousers they walked back to the pebble beach and the pine wood beyond it.

They were woken by two shrieking children running down to the water in plastic bathing shoes. They splashed each other and wrestled until both fell over and came up again, spluttering.

In silence Josip and Haris watched the two clowning, shrieking little boys who had the whole beach to themselves. Their high voices cut through the quiet air as their bodies wrinkled the smooth water.

Josip supported his back with his hands and turned to Haris, who was watching the children through a curtain of sleep-tousled curls. 'We're growing old,' said Josip. 'Two ugly old men, unwashed, unshaven, with back pains, tired.'

'Yes, we're growing old,' Haris agreed.

Together they shook out their blankets and went in turn to the lavatories in a beach pavilion, where they cleaned their teeth. There was a tempting smell of coffee but they did not order. The little money they had left was being kept for a different purpose.

'Shall we take the bus today for the sake of your back?' asked Haris.

Josip thought it over. 'Just one way, then.'

'And the rucksacks? Shall we hide them?'

'No, we'll take them with us this time. It might help. I mean if we assume we're going to find them, we shall find them sooner.'

'That's Mila logic,' said Haris.

'Poor, poor Mila,' said Josip.

They lifted the heavy rucksacks and went to the bus stop where, early as it was, some people were already waiting. Some of them frowned when they saw the boys and all of them tried not to sit too close to them. So at least they had enough space on the bus.

'Now you know what you have to look like to keep the muggers away!' said Haris.

'Once you've been mugged a few times this is the way you look,' said Josip.

Haris laughed. 'Very witty. My influence, I bet!' Grinning, they looked through the dusty windows at the pine trees between the beach and the road. 'Grill', 'Pizzeria', 'Pension', 'Mini-Golf', the notices flashed by, as if in a language that had fallen into disuse. And before them lay Split, with its shipyards and cement factories, its palms and its old centre. Millions of human feet had polished the pavements in the town until they gleamed like satin. Split felt like a carpet under their feet.

They got out at the harbour and looked at each other.

'What shall we do?' asked Haris. 'Shall we go to the market or the Gate? Or do you want to register first?'

'Telephone,' said Josip. 'Let's telephone again.'

They went to the post office and telephoned Sarajevo once more. But neither boy's parents could be reached. When they complained a post office official told them that their best chance of a connection would be with numbers that began with six.

'Have you got someone with a six in the family?' asked Haris.

'Not that I know of,' said Josip. 'But perhaps there's someone from school. Then we could call him and ask him to tell our parents that we're in Split. And after that we'll call him again and ask how they are.'

'Good idea,' said Haris, but he was scared. He loved his parents deeply, especially his father, whom everyone knew from television as a gentle man, but who was in reality hot-tempered and unpredictable. How often had Haris and his mother sat in the cellar when the town was being fired on, while his father went right on with his work up in the flat? Through the thunderous violence of the explosions, jumping at every crash, they had often wondered what made the man defy the guns with nothing more than blackout paper. Until one of them, his mother or he, ran upstairs to bring him down.

Their telephone number began with five, but, he remembered suddenly, the number of the Archaeological Museum began with six! The opening times had probably not changed at all, or very little. His father was a man who would if necessary act as attendant, ticket-seller and director. Haris could have rung right away, but of course tomorrow would do just as well, or the day after. It was unfair to keep the number from Josip, but it was only a matter of a day or two.

Without discussing it, they had walked straight to the boulevard with the palm trees. A white UN jeep raced by. UN vehicles were always racing through the streets of Split, as if to make up for the sluggish tempo in Bosnia.

'Haris!' Josip gestured to him to stop, took out a coin, tossed it in the air, caught it and covered it with his other hand. 'Heads we go to the Iron Gate, tails to the market square. All right?'

They bent over the coin, banging their heads together. Tails! Rubbing their foreheads, they walked to the market square, passing on the way a hotel where they had already asked three times 'if our friends have been here'. 'No,' the manageress had said last time, adding grumpily, 'Why don't you find some new ones?'

They slowed down at the entrance. 'We'll leave this one out,' said Haris. 'She doesn't like us. She's a money-grubber.'

'After all, we don't look very appetizing,' said Josip, looking at his trousers. 'Let's go to the shops we've been to before.'

'No,' said the man at the fishmonger's.

'No,' said the man in the handbag shop.

'No,' said the ice-cream man, 'I'm sorry.'

'No,' said the shoemaker, 'or – wait, just a moment.' He turned to his workshop and shouted over his shoulder, 'Marija! Marija, for you!'

At the back of the shop a door opened and a short, slightly-built girl appeared. As she stepped out of the semi-darkness of the workshop into the sunshine Josip and Haris could see that she was older than they had thought.

'I am Marija,' she said shyly and quite superfluously. 'I saw you four days ago, or three, I can't remember.'

'Have they been here?' cried Josip loudly.

'Two girls!' shouted Haris.

'Aida and Mila!' cried Josip.

'Yes,' said Marija, 'I saw them myself. They were here yesterday, just before you!'

The boys took a deep breath and swallowed, as if they were eating the news. Then they let out a shout that made the people in the market square look round. They punched each other's shoulders, laughed, yelled and generally made a row, but there were tears in their eyes.

'I've got their address,' said Marija, who was growing more and more uncomfortable.

'Do they know about us?' asked Josip.

'Where we are?' Haris added.

'Well, it went a bit wrong, because they spoke to my mother and she knew nothing about it. But I rang them up and told them about you. They asked what you looked like. They were most awfully worried. Shall I get the number? They are at the Jadran motor camp site.'

The shoemaker thought it was time for him to chip in: 'Do you want to telephone? There's a telephone in the passage.'

Josip and Haris hesitated, turning redder every moment.

'Marija!' called the shoemaker, 'what have you done with that number?'

The girl came back with a piece of paper which she presented to the now silent boys like a precious gift.

Haris read the address. 'We… we'll go there!'

Josip nodded. 'Yes, we'll surprise them.'

'It's nicer than 'phoning,' said Haris.

Marija looked quite disappointed now that she was going to miss the happy ending.

'Off you go,' said her father gruffly, 'you go to the bus

stop with them and tell them where to get off.'

There was something positively rude about the way they
took to their heels. They raised their hands, quite shamed
by the girl who waved to them on the departing bus. She
stood there like a little sailor's wife waving to her
menfolk. The boys turned away from the window, stared
straight ahead and sighed. Neither of them had known
how to explain their fears, without telling the whole
story of Ramiz.

At every place where they had left their names in Split,
they had always thought of Mila. In the end they had
stopped pretending and simply said that they came from
the Gora, which had earned them a little respite. If they
found the girls they could still tell the whole story, but
the shoemaker's daughter had innocently passed on the
truth and now they were worried about Mila. They
remembered her squabbles with Ramiz on the Gora. It
had been obvious from the beginning how fond they
were of each other, but also how hopelessly depressive
Ramiz had become.

By the time the bus stopped at the camp they were
exhausted with nervousness and tumbled out one after
another. While they were still standing at the bus stop,
the bus drove off. Haris was chewing his fingernails, Josip
massaging his back, and they were peering like thieves at
the wood in which dozens of caravans stood. Haris
stopped biting his nails. 'Come on, we have to tell them
some time, and they already know the worst.'

'I'm not going to start asking for them at every
caravan.'

'Here's an office,' said Haris. 'We'll ask there. Come

on!' He gripped Josip by the upper arm and urged him along to the entrance.

Three people were working in the office, a ventilator whirred, lifting pieces of paper, but providing no cool air at all. Apart from the quiet whirring and the tapping of a typewriter it was absolutely quiet. They leaned against the counter and waited until a man got up and asked if he could help.

'We have been looking for two Bosnian girls for a week now,' said Haris. 'They're probably here. Their names are Aida Osmić and Mila Stanišević.'

The man picked up a list and ran his finger down the names. 'Aida Osmić is here, yes, but we don't know the other one.'

The boys stared at each other. At last Josip managed to swallow down the lump in his throat. 'She must be here too! She is here!' he said reproachfully.

Haris nudged him.

'There are two of them!' said Josip. 'Aida isn't alone!'

'That's possible,' said the man, 'but when they have different surnames it's not easy for me to know if they're together.'

'Where is Aida?' asked Haris.

'Caravan fifty-two.'

'Is she living there on her own?'

'No. Go and have a look. She lives there with Samira Junuz and... Greta Muk.'

'But that's impossible!' cried Josip.

Haris thanked the man quickly and pushed his friend out of the office. 'Get looking!' he ordered. 'Find out how the numbers run and help to find the caravan!'

Because they were over-excited they lost their way once or twice, but in the end they saw the caravan, small and white, like the others. The door was open.

'I'm scared to go in,' said Haris, taking off his rucksack and sitting down on the ground. Josip copied him: he too didn't trust himself to go in. They watched the door anxiously and jumped when someone came out. It was Aida.

'Aida!' cried Josip, running towards her and doing without thinking what he had lacked the courage to do in Brodište. He took her in his arms and covered her face with kisses.

She yelled. 'Oh, Josip… boys!' The next moment she was being hugged and cuddled by Haris as well.

While they were jumping around each other like Balkan circle-dancers, Mila appeared on the little step. She looked deathly pale, but she was laughing.

Josip and Haris calmed down and stared at her in silence. Then they rushed to the steps, put their arms round Mila and held her close.

# Chapter 19

Ana, the camp manager, organized a tent for the two boys so that for the first time in ten days they had a roof over their heads. While Josip and Haris showered, Aida and Mila carried the rucksacks to the tent and blew up the airbeds. Then they waited. At last they could talk to each other in peace.

It turned out that Josip and Haris had reached the coast much earlier than Aida and Mila. Soon after the girls had written the letters the boys had read them and left the Gora. They had only just set out when Pedro overtook them.

'Pedro?' asked Aida, surprised. 'So he kept his word. Did he drive through Brodište?'

'Yes, and he had a row with his men over it,' said Haris with a smile. 'But he insisted. They were no longer an attraction to bandits, they had no supplies. In Brodište he found Antonia's house deserted and the furniture smashed, which gave him an awful shock. If he had been on his own, he told us, he would have gone up the Gora to look for Antonia. But the other Blues wanted to go on – all they did was help bury Napoleon. The dog was lying dead on the terrace. Pedro dug him a grave in the orchard. He couldn't stand the dog, but he knew how much Antonia loved it.'

While Haris was talking Aida tried to read Josip's face. Both of them had lost weight and looked tired and unwell. But at least Haris was talking, while Josip said nothing at all. 'Did you tell Pedro what had happened?'

'Yes, in our poor school French, but he understood the whole thing,' said Haris.

'And you?' asked Aida, 'did you go and look round again in Antonia's house?'

'No,' said Josip unexpectedly. 'Haris wanted to, but I didn't.'

Aida pointed to the caravan, which they could see from the tent. 'I've got something else for you, Josip. I don't know if it's the best one, but I like it. Wait a moment.' She ran to the caravan and came back with a photograph which showed Josip's aunt standing, laughing, in front of a school building.

Josip looked first at the picture and then at her. 'That's fantastically kind of you, really! But you shouldn't have gone back into that house!'

'I just picked it up. It was lying on top, by the window.'

There was a silence. Aida had told them how she and Mila had travelled from Brodište to Split, and Haris had reported how he and Josip had reached the coast. But there was something they had talked round, had not dared to mention, and now it was beginning to force itself on them. Mila, sitting like a statue at the back of the tent, asked no questions. She waited.

It was not Haris but Josip who spoke again, 'Mila, you know why Ramiz is not with us? Don't make us say it first. You do know, don't you, Mila?'

She nodded. 'He is dead.'

'Yes,' the boys whispered.

'I knew it,' said Mila, 'but it's better to know for certain.'

The silence after that was different, more honest and less tense. All four thought about the unlucky Ramiz.

'After they caught us,' Haris began, 'they took us to

the Planina, the mountain by the village of Izvor, where they had their camp. Our hands were tied and we were shut up in a hut, Josip, Ramiz and I together. That was what saved us, because it meant we could work something out. If we were honest, we hadn't the ghost of a chance. For three boys it wasn't worth the trouble to send for a car and get us taken to prison. They would probably have shot us if they had known where we came from. So the only possibility was to act as if we were Serbs. I was to say that my father kept an inn, Josip's father was the barman, and Ramiz's father a musician. The three of us had gone to Brodište to help my uncle and aunt but we hadn't found them and were very worried. Had all the Serbs been driven out?

'The disadvantage of our story was that it amounted to reporting for military service, but we couldn't think of anything better. With your hands tied behind your back you are powerless against two hundred men, roughly the number they had there. Josip was to be called Boris, I was Miso and Ramiz was Ramiz. He was actually the only one who could go on being himself. We had only just agreed on all this when a man came to fetch us – one by one, as we feared. Josip was the first. He came back half an hour later and I had no chance to ask how he had got on because I was the second. They began with Ramiz's hand, the one thing we had not discussed. They had recognized the type of injury and asked who had done it. I had no idea what Josip might have said, and I was pouring sweat. I said it had happened on the way, we had been attacked and Ramiz could no longer play the guitar, but he could shoot, he was strong, and certainly not soft. After that I told them some nonsense about my

175

father's inn and the songs I had heard there. I said that our mothers had thought we should still go to school and were too young for the army, but we thought differently. I don't know if they believed me, but fortunately they kept their hands to themselves. They had hit us in Brodište, now they seemed confused. I suppose they had been looking forward to putting a couple of boys through the hoop. If war is your profession, you take up some peculiar hobbies…

'But our story was a good one. It turned out later that we had said the same thing about the hand, apart from a few details. When Ramiz came back from his interrogation his hand had been dressed, which was a good sign. But we were not released. After two days a man came in who had been in Antonia's house. He asked about her slivovitz. I said my uncle Jovo was not only the best dentist but also the best slivovitz-maker in Brodište. He had felt that if he could not help people directly, there must at least be slivovitz on hand. It would help to dull the toothache, too. And I gave away the hiding-place for the slivovitz supply, which the man appreciated.

'I didn't invent what I said about Jovo, it was what Antonia had told me. I thought: I must get us out of here. If necessary we can learn to shoot. If things got serious we'll run away.

'Gradually they began to trust us. First they took the rope off our wrists so that we could sleep peacefully and undo our trousers without help.

'Then they left the door of the hut open. We could have left that scruffy dump, probably an old sheep pen, and run away. Josip did suggest it, but with two hundred men asleep all over the slopes I didn't dare to. I thought they were testing us and if we ran away they would shoot us down. If we stayed we would have proved ourselves as faithful comrades-in-arms. We just had to keep it up longer than they did, and then we could run for it when they forgot about us. That was my plan. But Josip was finding it more difficult to control his nerves every day and Ramiz was becoming more depressed by the hour. We were becoming less and less like boys who were longing to fight, and more and more like prisoners.

'At that point we had our first shooting practice behind us. Man, was I scared that Josip was going to aim at our instructor! "It's going well," I said that evening, "they're busy training us. We shall have a chance to get away. You must just hang on for a little while. We don't do anyone any harm, we eat what we ate on the Gora and we only shoot at targets." I expected problems with Josip, but he agreed.

'It was Ramiz who could not stand it any longer. His hand was inflamed again and he had had enough. One evening, perhaps the eighth or ninth day on the Planina, he told us, "This way is taking too long. You must go back to the Gora and help Aida and Mila. As soon as I have an opportunity to distract the men, get going!" We were very scared. "How about you?" we asked.

'"I don't want to go on," Ramiz said. "I'm nothing without music."

'We went on arguing with him until it was light, telling him he was talking rubbish. Then we fell asleep. Ramiz picked up his rifle – we already had our own weapons – crept out of the hut and fired off a salvo into the air and in all directions. The entire camp started running about, trying to find out what had happened.

'Josip and I knew, but we could not help him. He had helped us... if we hurried! So we rushed down the mountain and were already some distance away when we saw them shoot him down. He can't have suffered at all, it was over so fast. We ran to the Gora at once without going back to the village, so we didn't see what they had done there. I assume they behaved like any boozers who find their boozing place shut. Up on the Gora we found your letter. First one, then two, then three, then four, and then five – and all the same. We hung them like a garland over our beds. We stayed for a day or so, to pack up and rest, then we set off, on your trail.'

Mila had not moved. She was still sitting straight-backed, her legs crossed. For Haris her reaction could not have been worse. He pushed his fingers through his curls, which immediately fell over his face again, long and thick as they now were.

'Haris,' said Josip, 'the letter. Give her Ramiz's letter!'

'Oh yes,' said Haris. 'He wrote a letter. Shall I get it out, Mila?'

'You don't need to ask,' said Aida. 'Get it, stupid.'

Haris got his rucksack and took a tightly folded piece of paper from one of the pockets. 'Here you are,' he said quietly.

It was an envelope, which the boys had found by the rubbish tip on the Planina. Ramiz had scrawled a brief message with his sound left hand. The others watched in silence as Mila opened it and read it through, three times or more.

*Dear Mila,*

*Forgive me. I couldn't take it. Try to understand. I would*

*always have been moody, and someone like you deserves*
*something better. If you see my father and mother, ask them too*
*to forgive me. I hope I was able to help Josip and Haris a little*
*bit. Don't be sad, it's better this way. Do your best to be happy.*
*Love, Ramiz*

Mila folded the letter slowly, like a document that might fall apart. Then she crawled out of the tent. 'It's not your fault, Haris. It's what he wanted, you know that. If I see his father and mother I'll tell them everything, and if I see my father and mother I shall set fire to their inn. And if I see my brothers I shall lynch them! I'm going to bed. Good night.'

The three who were left gazed at each other, shaken. 'Has she been like this long?' asked Haris.

'Since yesterday,' said Aida. 'Since she knew that Ramiz was not with you. First she had a good cry, and I thought: now it's coming out. But when she was quieter and calmer she started on her parents. She said the strangest things. She talked about the revenge of the Terrible Gypsy. What she meant by that I don't know.'

'Revenge,' murmured Haris. 'How could she ever avenge Ramiz? Revenge would only hurt her. Revenge is self-destructive, my father says.'

'Hm.' Aida pursed her lips. When suffering reached a degree that you could no longer bear, it exacted its toll on the people who caused it. Mila's fury she could understand, but not her sarcasm. 'She just jokes, she's so cynical,' she told the boys.

'She's ill,' said Josip suddenly. 'Leave her to sort herself out. How long has she known now? One day! Let her work it off and make wicked plans. She won't carry them

179

out, it will just help her to recover. "Greta Muk" – was that her idea?'

'Yes,' said Aida.

The three of them had to laugh as they looked across through the open tent entrance to the caravan, where a single feeble light was burning.

'She really is a great girl!' said Haris.

The others nodded in the darkness.

With sudden decision Aida sat down on the floor of the tent between the beds. She shook out the pillows and opened the sleeping bags. 'I'm sending you to bed!' She looked on with satisfaction as the two freshly-washed boys crawled in. With strands of damp hair hanging over their foreheads and only their noses peeping out of their sleeping-bags they looked ten years younger – like two seven year-olds, she thought.

With a sudden inspiration she leaned over them and gave each of them a goodnight kiss. First Haris, then Josip, a fraction longer. 'Sleep well!'

'Good night,' came the chorus of two already sleepy voices as she closed the zip on the tent entrance.

She walked over to the caravan, in which the woman, rolled up like a snail, was already asleep. At the other end, where the light was burning, lay Mila. Aida quickly took off her shorts and pulled her jersey over her head. She was going to switch off the light when Mila unexpectedly turned over. 'No, leave it on! I'm frightened!'

Shocked, Aida laid a hand on her hammering heart. 'I thought you were asleep. What are you afraid of?'

'Such dreadful things are going through my head! I don't know where they come from. All these ideas. They come of their own accord.'

'What sort of ideas?'

'Oh no!' whispered Mila. 'If I talk about them they'll just get worse.' She pushed herself up to look at Aida, despair in her dark eyes.

'Worse ideas than the one you've already told me about?'

'Much worse. Dreadful ideas!'

Aida lay down, her hands behind her head. 'Mila, everyone has horrible ideas at some time or another. Josip talked about evil plans, but those plans come of their own accord. Suddenly they're there, that's why they're so scary. As for me...'

'Were you talking about me?'

'Yes, just briefly, in the tent.'

'What did you say?'

Sighing, Aida poured some water. 'Oh, Mila, don't get so worked up! We're always your friends. Come on, drink up.'

'What did you say?'

'I said that I was worried about you, Josip said you must let off steam, it would do you good, and Haris said you were a great girl.'

Surprise seemed to make Mila's teeth chatter on the glass as she drank, but she was noticeably calmer. Her body became relaxed and heavy until, with her arms round Aida, she fell asleep.

Aida was not comfortable, but she didn't move and only when Mila's breathing turned into a soft snore alternating with a high whistle did she release herself from the clinging arms and fall asleep exhausted.

# Chapter 20

Now Haris felt up to it! You do feel braver after a good sleep. The four of them were standing in the town post office.

'Go on then, dial the number!' Josip encouraged him.

Haris nodded. If the Archaeological Museum had not been damaged by shells or mortars and his father was not injured, the call was bound to get through. His hands were shaking as he dialled the number.

'Well?' asked Josip.

'It's ringing, ssshh!'

'What now?'

'Still ringing. Do be quiet!'

At last someone answered: 'Archaeological Museum, good morning,' said a woman's voice – or was it a tape?

Haris was sweating. 'Is... my father... Edin Musanović, still there?' It was a very direct, but also ambiguous question, which exactly reflected what he was feeling.

A click on the line. 'Just a minute.'

'Yes, hallo,' he heard suddenly. 'Musanović here.'

Haris shuddered. All at once he had goose pimples all over his body. 'Pap!' he shouted. 'Is it you? Haris, Haris here! We're in Split, Josip and I. How are you and Mama?'

The others tried to make out what his father was saying from Haris's face and uninformative answers. 'Yes. No. Really? No, everything's all right. Yes. Good.'

Finally it was Josip who could no longer control himself. 'How are things at my home?' he cried, but jumped when Haris handed him the receiver.

'Take it, man!' said Haris.

'Josip here.'

'Hallo Josha!' said Haris's father. 'It's all right, my boy, your parents are well. A bit tense, a bit thin, but nobody's suffering from obesity in these parts nowadays. They and we are well, but the house is not. We have had mortar hits in the entrance and a fire immediately afterwards, and there's not much left. Fortunately we were in the cellar. We have now moved with all the books, pictures and clothes we could save to the service flat in the museum, with your parents. The flat is further from the hills, which makes it safer. Don't you worry! Look, I've suggested to Haris somewhere you could go. Think it over. Your parents are not at home, no. Could you ring again, now you know where we are? Your mother is getting better slowly, Josha, and this call will do her good!'

Josip thanked him and returned the receiver to Haris. 'Pap,' he heard his friend saying casually, 'do you know, we've seen some fabulous *stećci*! A field full of them, at Brodište, on the southern slopes of the Gora. Every kind of shape and symbol you can imagine. I tried to clean them up, but I had no tools. As soon as it's possible again we'll go and have a look, right? What? Twelve tons, I should think, at least… No, not at present… Yes, I'll do that. All my love to Mama!'

Haris rang off. The relief in his haggard face was infectious and his eyes were shining. 'They're alive,' he said, laughing. 'They're still alive, all four of them!'

They strolled back to the beach. Haris would have liked to run and jump for joy, but restrained himself in front of the girls. Aida could not ring home and Mila had

184

no intention of doing so. But the growing need to give physical expression to his relief was not satisfied by the peaceful stroll. He walked faster and faster and when he saw a fountain he gave in to the first thought that entered his head. Stepping into the basin, he began to trot round and round like a horse through a veil of water. They watched him, open-mouthed.

'Have you gone crazy?' asked Josip. 'No, I was hot,' came a voice they could scarcely make out above the splashes. 'Is it cold?' asked Josip. 'Fresh!' they heard him shout back. Grinning, Josip sat on the edge and then also climbed into the basin, turned his face to the jets of water and shouted an exaggerated, 'Brrrrrr!' All the children who had stopped, fascinated, began to laugh at the two boys who were pretending to clean their teeth, wash themselves, or chase each other. The adults shook their heads. At first Aida and Mila had looked on, embarrassed, but now they too were sitting on the edge of the basin, egging the boys on. A passer-by got annoyed when he was hit by a stream of water; a mother had problems with her little boy – who also wanted to get in with all his clothes on – and a dog raced round and round, barking and snapping at the flying drops of water.

They did not see where the policeman came from. Suddenly he was there, ordering Haris and Josip to get out of the fountain. They stood before him, shivering and dripping wet. The children moved closer to hear what he would say.

'What's going on?' asked the policeman. 'Isn't the sea big enough for you?'

Josip opened his mouth. His lips were blue with cold. But Haris was ahead of him: 'Sir... sir,' he said, as stiff with cold as his friend, 'we, we have just rung Sarajevo and heard that our parents are all right!'

The policeman shook the boys by the hand, a gesture that many of the bystanders seemed to find incomprehensible.

So the four of them walked on, leaving behind them a trail of water which vanished at once in the heat of the September sun.

'Have we got any money left?' asked Haris. Pedro had given him and Josip a small amount and Ana had given some to Aida and Mila. But the telephone call had been expensive, and the bus tickets as well.

Mila opened her purse. 'No, we're nearly broke.'

'Have we got enough to go and drink something?' asked Haris, nodding his head towards the café gardens along the boulevard.

'Yes, just about,' said Mila, 'but you must get dry before you start ordering drinks.' She twitched at his clothes. She was far from being the old Mila, but there were moments when she seemed to be moving in that direction.

Josip went over to Aida and put an icy hand on the back of her neck. 'And me, have I got to wait too before having something hot to drink?'

She shot away with a shriek, only to return, laughing. She took his hand and rubbed it between her own. 'Does that help, Josha?'

'Much better than the sun!'

'Ha!' said Haris. 'Sir wants a bit of cosseting!' He looked challengingly at Aida, who blushed and turned away.

'Two teas and two cokes,' Mila ordered.

The two boys were not dry yet and they sat, pale and numbed, on the wicker patio chairs, but they hadn't wanted to wait any longer.

Aida smiled as they clasped their fingers round the hot glasses and put their noses into the circling steam. The sun set, round and red, reminding all of them of past holidays, when the languages they heard were not spoken by soldiers in civilian clothes, but by Spanish, English and French tourists. The white vehicles that tore past were ambulances. The holes in the road signs were not bullet holes but normal corrosion, a result of the salt in the air. And the overcrowded camp sites and pensions were all part of the holiday season. Who didn't like going to the seaside?

And they themselves, they were two girls and two boys who liked each other and were spending their pocket money on drinks. Aida thought of the mountains from which she and her mother had sometimes seen the sea. Mila sniffed at the roses that surrounded the terrace, smelling again the holidays of her childhood. And Josip saw himself in memory racing with a fanatical neighbour boy to be first to the sea.

So they were quite startled when Haris brought them back to reality with one sentence, 'We can't stay here, of course. My father advises us to go north. We have family there.'

Mila reacted more fiercely than the others. 'Oh, and why can't we stay?'

'Just try to imagine it. The two of you with a stranger in one caravan, the two of us in a tent, all winter, without work, with nothing to do. We can't even go to school.'

'There is a sewing course,' said Mila.

187

Haris fell on his knees at her feet. 'Mila, you can skin rabbits, milk goats, bake bread, build huts, you've already proved that to us. Don't take us for fools. Of course you can also sew and knit and embroider, weave carpets, hang wallpaper, clean chimneys and repair televisions! Nothing you did would surprise us. You don't need courses, you need work, otherwise you will be bored to tears. And if you're bored you go crazy.'

'They've been waiting for me all this time, in the north, all those Croats!'

Haris laughed. 'For people like you, sure! My uncle and aunt have a discotheque between Split and Zadar. My father says they're making a small profit at last.'

'And then we turn up?' asked Josip.

'We have hands, we can do something, can't we? And we'll stay close enough to home to ring up from time to time.'

Haris was sitting down again, because his theatrical pose, on his knees before Mila, was attracting attention.

Silently they thought it over, drinking away the last of their money in small sips. They would have to go back on foot.

'But Haris,' said Aida, 'you didn't tell your father anything about Mila and me. When he advised you to go north he meant Josip and you. It makes quite a difference to your uncle and aunt, taking in two lodgers or four.'

Haris tossed back his curls and forced her to look a him, bitter reproach in his eyes. 'My father's not alone either, is he? He has my mother and she has him. So Josip and I can get to know people as well. I got to know you, and he to know Mila, for instance, or vice versa.'

Josip shook his head and gave Mila a worried look, but it was not really about him or her.

Aida bowed her head and said nothing. She was staring at her toes, which were getting sunburned since Mila had cut out the toecaps of her shoes.

'Shall we pay now?' asked Josip. 'We've got quite a long way to walk.'

They nodded, leaned back and waited for the waiter. On the way back to Jadran Aida walked with Mila.

It was still September when they set off for Grana, the old fishing town where Haris's family lived.

It was a busy place, but in a different way from Split. There were genuine tourists here! And tourists, they noticed, did not walk about in the same way as other people. They looked more closely at their surroundings than the inhabitants, but also with the disinterest of people who come, and go away again.

On the one hand the sight of people loafing about reassured them; on the other hand it infuriated them. They stared, frowning, at the surfboards, canoes and pedalos and the foreign buses with their loads of French and German tourists. 'We'll get used to it,' said Josip.

If Haris's uncle and aunt found their four guests a burden they hid it well. The boys were given an attic room and the girls one below. The quickest to adapt was Mila; Haris's relations were delighted with her. They were soon calling her 'the girl with the golden hands'. They themselves were childless and well over forty, but all their dream children looked just like Mila.

'I might stay here,' said Mila one night.

Aida was shocked. 'Won't you ever go home then?'

'When I've got the strength, when I haven't got these dreadful ideas, I might visit them once, perhaps. What about you, are you going back to Tuz?'

'What would I do in Tuz? Everyone I knew has gone. All my friends, all my relations. I only have you three.'

'Hey… you're in love with Josha, aren't you?'

'How did you know?'

Mila laughed. 'I've known for quite a time, but whether he knows is another matter. Why are you so stuffy with him?'

'It's difficult, Mila. It's to do with Haris. I don't want Haris and Josip to quarrel over me.'

'Does it help to know that Haris and I like each other?'

Aida switched on the light and surveyed Mila. 'How do you mean, "like"?'

'Very much!' said Mila. 'Really very much! Sometimes I suffer over Ramiz, and of course Haris is quite different. He's dominant, he's strong, but I can just be dominant back.'

Aida lay down again, nonplussed. 'Why haven't I noticed anything?'

'It's only just started,' said Mila. 'But I saw it coming for weeks. Why don't you behave differently to Josip tomorrow? Not so snappy, I mean. Haris is a play-actor, he acts off his insecurity. But Josip, the good soul, can't do that.'

'What a goose I am!' said Aida.

'We are all geese. I promised Haris that I would go to the Gora with him as soon as it's safe there. And that I would finally take the time to have a look at the *stećci*.'

'But you thought they were gruesome, didn't you?'

'There are more gruesome things than stones, aren't there? And what I've heard about the Bogomils fascinates me. I must know where the evil comes from, if I'm to believe in something good again.'

## *Glossary*
### (including pronunciation)

| | |
|---|---|
| balija | term of abuse for Muslims |
| C, c | pronounced *ts* |
| ć, Ć | pronounced *tsh* |
| Č, č | pronounced *ch* |
| Chetnik | Serbian nationalist |
| djuveć | rice dish |
| gusle | one-stringed instrument |
| icon | portrait of saint in eastern Orthodox church |
| Jedan peva drugi svira | one sings, the other plays (from gypsy song) |
| kafana | bar room of an inn |
| khoja | pronounced *hodja*: Islamic teacher |
| kolodans | circle dance, in which the participants hold hands |
| mujaheddin | fundamentalist Muslim guerrillas |
| papaks | Serbs besieging Sarajevo |
| polje | field, plain |
| Š, š | pronounced *sh* |
| Serbofor | derogatory nickname for UNPROFOR |
| stara groblja | old graveyard |
| stećak, stećci | Bogomil stones (singular and plural) |
| UNPROFOR | UN peace-keeping force in former Yugoslavia |
| Ustasha | Croat nationalist |
| Ž, ž | pronounced j |